ANGELS
WHISPER YOU'RE NOT CURSED
Galations 5:1

VICTORIA MOORE

Angels Whisper You're Not Cursed

This book is written to provide information and motivation to readers. Its purpose is not to render any type of psychological, legal, or professional advice of any kind. The content is the sole opinion and expression of the author, and not necessarily that of the publisher.

Copyright © 2024 by Victoria Moore.

Printed in the United States of America.

ISBN   xxx-x-xxxxx-xxx-x   (Paperback)
ISBN   xxx-x-xxxxx-xxx-x   (Digital)

Lettra Press books may be ordered through booksellers or by contacting:

Lettra Press LLC
30 N Gould St. Suite 4753
Sheridan, WY 82801
1 307-200-3414 | info@lettrapress.com
www.lettrapress.com

TABLE OF CONTENTS

I Was Cursed

I wrote this chapter years before Chapter 1. My life was completely different, my "guardian angel" was still in my life as well as all the other "accusers." My thinking was different too. I believed myself cursed, a victim of my circumstances. I saw myself as an ugly monster, and I saw no future or hope for me. This chapter reads like a soliloquy. I decided to leave it because I do not want to forget who I once was and who I have become now. I am now me because of Jesus and I am not cursed. But I am jumping ahead.

We dream so many wonderful dreams when we are children, having no idea what the future has determined for us. Our dreams are perfect, and our hopes are reachable. We jump like Michael Jordan with no holds barred like Shaq. The wisdom we glean when we are forty years older looking back.

Dear Self,

I am writing this letter to you in hopes you will one day look back and be amazed at all the answered prayers. There is too much about us that no one will ever know except father, and of course, our guardian angel. But I do not think anyone knows the whole story about us. Even our guardian angel, he knows more than anyone else, but not everything. Can I remind you of a memory so long ago that determined the rest of our future? We were in the church sanctuary at Dale City Christian Church. You were sitting on the piano stool with Gabriel messing around on the piano and giggling. It was after "the thing" and after Jacob had popped "the question" for the fourth time. Gabriel stopped playing and quietly whispered, "marry me." Do you remember that day? Of course, you do, we rehearsed it to exhaust whenever things got depressing, deep in the midnight hours. We replayed that day over and over like a broken record. You never gave him an answer, but that day changed the rest of our lives. You needed someone to love you, instead you chose men like your dad, men who lacked love for you and all the love for themselves. You spent your life chasing love. It would take love to find you. One day you will let love find you and when you do, do not let it go. I love you, Self.

Sincerely, Vicky

Fea! Fea! The kids loved to call me that, throwing pennies in my hair and spitballs in my face. The word "fea" in Spanish means "ugly." Some of the boys would stick out their feet and trip me, face first, into the hard-cold linoleum floors of the school, and the crowd of kids would burst out laughing. I do not know how many times per year my glasses would get broken or I would have a busted lip. "You're so ugly, your mama doesn't want you," one of the boys would chide to keep the class laughing. The teachers would sit behind books and pretend not to see or hear. They did not want to get involved. Silently I would pick myself up and collect my dropped things and continue my way down the hall to class. I was ugly: large, black-rimmed glasses hid two large almond-shaped brown eyes with dark black wrinkled circles under them from excessive crying. I had large, dry lips and a big nose that took up most of my face, combined with big eyes and large front teeth. I was as thin as a rail and languished over the fear of turning out like a boy. But I had the thickest bushy black hair a mother could ever have the dread of taming. My mom gave me two or three lop-sided braids that stuck out from my head until they grew long enough to go down my back. And even then, they looked like black tusks coming from my head.

I never spoke one word outside my parents' home, not one. My lips were sealed; I was quiet and wordless until I got inside my house. It was not that I could not talk; I was very talkative around people I knew. I just chose not to talk around people I did not know. This made me even more of a freak to the kids at school.

The one thing that opened my mouth was music. When I opened my mouth and sang a song, even the cruelest kid would stop hurting me for the moment and listen. You could hear my sadness in every line; it was a soulful, melodic melodrama that soared strongly and loudly all around me and anyone else in earshot. Music was my power. Most adults said they could not believe the sound that came out of my little body. It was like Ella Fitzgerald and Dinah Washington had crammed themselves inside of me. I was five years old when I first began to sing. The song that became my claim to fame at the time was Showboats: *Can't Help Loving That Man of Mine.* The graduating class of '86 requested for me to sing the song leading the school choir. The drama was in my voice (easily gleaned from the drama and abuse that grew fertile in my home, spilling over into school), and my face and body acted out the words; however, the verses did not need me to perform them. My voice spoke what I was incapable of saying myself, and the sound. That sound. I never needed a microphone, only music. When I sang, I could see on the faces of those around me the awe of the sound that came powerfully out of me, and it was like a surge of a high. Crack could not compare, and meth could not touch this high that music gave. It was my Wonder Woman bangles. When I got caught up in a song, even my father's rages melted away; the hate from the kids at school became nothing.

Later in life, I would sing at a venue in Washington, DC, with my band, the Praise Band. I was not the lead singer, but that night I had a chance to sing a solo. There were many important people in the audience. We were honoring the homeless and vets. That evening the building was packed, standing room only. Our goal was to raise money for the shelter there. I sang "Amazing Grace" acapella. In usual form, I looked straight above the heads of the crowd and sang to Him who meant all to me.

I felt enveloped by the music and it carried me away. There was not a dry eye in the house. It was like I was just sitting and listening to me sing; no one else in the room. When I finished and scanned the room, I saw rows of tears, smiles, and awed faces confronting their maker. I could not hear the applause when the room returned from nirvana, only the strong desire to run from the stage. Maria and Terry came up on either side of me, and we continued singing with "O the Deep Deep Love of Jesus" as a quartet acapella at first, and then later with the instrumentation. Going to that mountain high was magical. It was nights like this that I forgot who I was, where I lived, and what I would be going home to. I forgot that I was Fea; I was a singer. "Amazing Grace" would become a signature song for me through the years.

Repeatedly throughout my life I would fall victim to an unhealthy passion for mean men. My life was the stuff of campy country songs. It has been a melodrama Hollywood could not imagine how to pen. From the afternoon that Jacob came home from Desert Storm on the wooden planks of the shipyard at Andrews Air Force Base, where hours later, he'd hit me for the first time, knocking me off the bed and onto the floor, then shaking me insisting that we "do it" because he needed it or I would get more of what just happened; to the love of my life, Gary, charging down the hill of his front lawn in anger calling me a nigger, threatening to kill me and screaming for my ugliness to leave and get out of his face. The stuff of tragic plays, my life.

And yet, I met four presidents, sang on the White House lawn, the lawn of DC on the Fourth of July,

Kennedy Center, Patriot Center, Wolf Trap, and the Hilton Chapel, just to name a few. Sometimes it was with prestigious choirs, and other times in solo, wearing gorgeous gowns, and later in life, beautiful wigs. You never knew that behind every show was a man waiting to scream in my face; an ugly finger; threatened destitution, pain, or worse; a large hand coming down to slap the make-up off my face; a foot kicking the guts out of me; a fist anxiously punching my shoulder or gut; a fist penetrating my heart mercilessly (night after night being raped by the one who vowed to love me). I stayed trapped in what could be an addiction to cruel men, because I did not want to be alone. I did not want to be forgotten. I wanted to be loved, and if pain would lead to one kind word, one warm hug, one thoughtful action, then it seemed worth it. I learned to compartmentalize all of it.

I lived one life as all music that I loved, with Pentecostal holiness fervor. It was all I did, in church, volunteering with my bands or choirs or solo. I had one life which was my everyday life as a quiet, kind gentle person trying to help someone; taking strays in and loving the unlovable; mothering my five little children (later to blossom to seven) and everyone else's little baby. Then there was the dark life: me the victim, waiting in fear for my husband to come home, hoping I could determine where he was at so this time I could make him happy, avoiding the violence that came when things did not go his way, or thinking of a plan to calm and soothe a boyfriend whom I clinged to for fear of being alone. I hoped that whatever favors I could give him (tug and rub) would make him stay one more day.

My voice was bewitching: a little girl's soft, gentle, tickling, playful voice that made men smile. I could milk a feeling in song to influence a person to give me a little bit of time. It was all I wanted, just time. Never forced, always sincere, filled with longing of not wanting to be alone. Men took it the wrong way; women thought me manipulative. Not many people get who I am. I am a child imprisoned inside this woman's body searching for my father and longing for my mother to come back, clinging to my siblings and anticipating hanging with my relatives in New York.

From when I was fifteen, I stopped growing up. There I stayed at fifteen. My mind never went past that threshold socially, even though my intelligence grew to be higher than most people. To the men I married, it was this character that drove them crazy and brought the impatient abusive behavior out of them. Out of these experiences with men (and women), a monster would be born inside of me, and it would hold me prisoner all my life, till I was set free. You can only kick a dog for so long before it begins to bite back. This unpredictable monster would dictate which way we would go down the road of life, how far my career would go, who would be allowed into my life, and who would not. And it was the suffocating control of this monster that would bring my guardian angel back into my life and keep him closer and closer to my side until he tried to close my life.

The monster made me a paradox. To those around me, I was warm, personable, kind, loving, giving, a people person, a strong woman, and highly intelligent; a strong presence you felt when I walked into the room. You knew

I was there. But the other side of me was cold, distant, a hater of humankind, angry, wounded, weak, and always with a sense of being lost among others, insecure and scared of everything around the corner, even though there was nothing there. I was in search for my prince to come save me, not recognizing he had come, and he had saved me, and He had never left me. I was blind until he opened my eyes.

I had few friends; in my younger years I had many friends before the monster had a hold of me. I loved talking and gossiping with my friends. I loved shopping in the mall, chatting away, and laughing like it was the best day of my life. I would search for people to become attached to that were like my mom or a big sister, or a strong brother or father-figure type person, and I felt complete and secure in their presence. If they were married, their husbands were my brothers and I felt even more complete, though at times, for some, it sent out the wrong signals and created misunderstanding. I made my family live through their families; I did not know how to have a family, and I did not want to be a single parent. I knew my home, when my husband came home, was a tornado of pain, so I lived vicariously through my friends. It was a form of survival, making the nightmare of home life bearable.

As the years went by and I got older, I pulled more into myself and away from friends, carving out family traditions of my own. I did not want anyone to know my home and what we lived with. I did anything to keep my husband satisfied even if I had to do "favors" during the day. I wanted my imaginary life I created by using my friends, more so than my life with Ken, Howard, or Jacob.

I "bought" freedom with food, money, clothes, "toys," favors; anything they wanted, I got; I did anything to keep their anger at bay (and I hated myself for it). Some things I had to do were humiliating, and I felt ashamed that I let myself stoop so low, but it bought me time to pretend my pretend life just a little longer.

My story is a story that has been told. It is not a tall tale made up; however, when you put all the parts together, it seems impossible, huge! How could it be that all this happened to one person, one woman. within a short life? I improved on my reality by lying to myself. I could not allow myself to believe my true life; it was too horrid from start to present. That is how I survived it all; fooling myself that the past did not exist. Even when I was questioned by the social worker about the bruises on my arm and neck and face, I still lied. I used heavy makeup on my arms and legs and neck to cover up old and new marks, but I still lied to myself and others. No matter how guarded I tried to be about the tragedies in my life that I could not talk about or reveal to others, my life was written on my face and in my eyes, and it was heard in the sound of my voice when I sang. There was no hiding the distinctive sound of pain and sorrow.

This is a book about the darkness. It is about the darkness that enveloped me and tried to destroy me repeatedly. It is about a brokenhearted girl who chased disaster repeatedly like an expensive diamond. I lived what the famous singers sing. I am no Cinderella. I waited for Prince Charming, and I thought he never came, like the fairy tale. He did not. I never found what I was looking for, my white knight like in the lullabies. Instead I got a sentinel and the love I always wanted and longed for, just not in the way I expected. I died piece-by-piece with every year that went by until my guardian found a way to stop the march of time and rewind the clock. He made time go back to where I stopped growing and caused it to stay there so I could begin living. I thought he would become "that man of mine." But his salvation came close to ending my life, had it not been for my Father.

> "When my father and my mother forsake
> me, then the Lord will take care of me."
> Psalm 27:10 (NKJV)

CHAPTER ONE

Where to Begin

It is very difficult to know where to start one's story. I had always planned to write the story of my life. I assumed I would one day be very famous on a stage entertaining millions of people through music. I knew this was my destiny from the time I was very little, and I held onto my love of singing and entertaining even when all of me wanted to crawl into the floor and hide away from the world forever. I truly believed I would be found like Marilyn Monroe and Lana Turner. I just needed to be in the right place at the right time. That was the hard part. Who comes to backwards Dale City, Virginia? This was truly the boonies when I was growing up. The likelihood of being discovered in this place was next to nil, yet I kept my hopes up. I had my hikes up to New York City and my summer jaunts up to Washington, DC, growing up. I assumed that one day a producer would see me and say, "Hey kid, you want to be a star?" and I would say "sure," and my life of fame and fortune would begin.

But life is not like a television sitcom where our problems are easily resolved within the thirty to forty-five minutes your story is playing over the airwaves. There are so many surprises, twists, and turns; situations that seem to make no sense and the constant gnawing of unresolved puzzles with no answers. Our lives are a play on the stage that God has created called life. He has written our story, and so He knows all the whos, whats, whens, wheres, hows, and whys. However, I am the one in the dark. It is this fact that leads so many of us to think God to be sadistic, uncaring, a child playing with us like a toddler plays with toys. We are left throughout our lives with so many unanswered questions, and we are thrown into a scramble daily trying to figure out the answers and put the pieces of the puzzle together, so we can breathe a deep, heavy sigh and feel the satisfaction of resolving the burdens in our lives that plague us till we die.

I am going to be honest with you; I hate this. At least actors on the stage in New York City are given a book with their lines and their stage blocking so they know what to say, how to feel, and where to move and stand. The director comes during practice and he may reinterpret a block here or a line there. He may give suggestions as to how you should feel or think and what your attitude should be to color the story just right. It makes life seem so easy to have someone help you know what to do and how to do it. Not life. In life, there is no playbook. We have no blocking and no lines, no suggestion of where to stand, what to do, or what to feel. The story is written from beginning to end; however, all the actors have no idea how the story is going to go or how it is going to end. We are all playing by ear. We make countless mistakes going down roads we should never go down, saying things we should never say, and affecting others around us in negative ways we never meant. But once it done, it is done.

Now that I have lived half a century, I can look back and wonder how, why, and what, and I can say, I do not understand. Nothing seems to fit together, and yet, everything fits together perfectly. This is not the story I would have determined for me to play. And, well, I am not dead yet. I am not close to being dead yet. So, of course, my story is not done. This play is only halfway through. I can say the first act is complete, and it seems right now I am in intermission. This is the point I can write and publish Act I, knowing very well that Act II will be written and completed another time. Someone else will probably write that story. Maybe I will be famous then. Maybe I will be gracing the stages of this planet with my presence throwing my large voice out into the audience with lyrical melodies that tickle the ears and warm the heart. I hope so. I am not dead yet, so I still have time to meet my dreams. Some of my dreams.

But back to this story. I do not want you to think I do not trust God with myself and my story. I do. I am not an atheist. And I am not lost in other faiths and ideologies, which I believe is man's attempt to run away from God and prove he can write his story better than God. No, I know who God is. But there are parts to my story where I think, really God, this really had to happen to me? I really had to live through this? This part was so important to add into my story and you could not do things in a different way? I mean there are mistakes in my life that if God the director had interpreted some of the parts to me before they had happened, I would have made some better choices, and so many would not be devastated and broken, myself included. As an example, did I really need to marry a criminal? Could you not tell me he was a criminal? Was it truly necessary for all of us to be abused by this man and remolded into broken people? Why this, God? Or how about the night I got a ride home from my manager from my job. Really God, rape? Was this honestly necessary? Did you have to build this wall into my life so that pursuit of my dreams would become a lifelong struggle with myself? Why, what are you accomplishing through this travesty?

But here is the classic showstopper: in that little Sunday school classroom crying my eyes out after Reverend Jones refused to marry Jacob and I, God, could you not come and talk to me in your still small voice? I was praying to you, for crying out loud. I was talking to you, asking for answers, directions. You could not give me some, just a little bit? Could you not say, "Michelle, run!" I would have obeyed you, Lord. I was ultra-spiritual back then, still on the new Christian honeymoon with you, wide-eyed and willing to do whatever you asked me to. That was the time to say "Michelle, run." I was listening to you. My heart was more open at that time than any other time in my life. I did not know bitterness, hate, confusion, abandonment, or emptiness then. You filled my life at that time. I saw nothing but Jesus. There are seven children who could have been spared so much unnecessary pain and loss. Two families that endured years of in-house fighting and cruel actions bordering on inhuman. The lives of so many shattered, mine included. All you had to do is say "Run, Vicky, run!" But then, that day, that Sunday schoolroom situation was the fork in the road of my life. This point determined who I would be and what story would be told of me. As much as I wish God had called my name with a bullhorn and yanked me out of that church that day, I would not be writing this story—and there would be no story to tell—had I not married Jacob Blowfish.

It was like that day I grew up. I became a woman. I was no longer a child. The night before, we were still children, and we acted so too. My mom put my wedding together with Dr. Banister. The night before, Jacob was in a minor car accident and dented his car. It was not safe for him to drive home, so he spent the night sleeping downstairs in my brothers' room. I hung out upstairs with my mom, my cousins, my grandmother, and Aunt Cocoa watching TV, laughing, eating food, and enjoying the impromptu family reunion. There is a picture of me laying across my brothers' bed in my blue and pink fluffy nightgown and house shoes, curled up in a fetal position, like any kid on any given evening. That same night Anabel, JoJo, and my brothers all got into another car accident on the ice too, going out for food. It was a strange and crazy night. My whole story could have been completely different had their car accident been major instead of minor yet scary. Or, if Jacob had died instead of walking away from his fender bender that night, I might never had gotten married, and my life story would be different. But it was not time for such life stirring tragedies yet. As a family, we had already lived through a few tragedies that had become taboo for us to speak of. At this time in my life, we focused on the future, and we ignored the past as if it never happened. It was a weird existence, but it was an unwritten understanding we all kept.

My parents' beginnings were completely different from mine and opposite of each other. God wrote a life story for both of my parents that made it seem impossible for these two to have ever met. If one moment in time had never happened, these two would never had met. If my father had not made one life-changing decision, my brothers and I would never had been born.

In every life story I go over as I write this book, I discover a repetitive pattern. There is always one moment in time that determines everyone's story. If that one moment did not happen, the stories of our lives would not exist. My conclusion from this is that God is the writer and the director of our story. He is not sitting back and quietly watching. I am not snatching the pen out of His hand and rewriting the story to my own liking. I cannot. Even when God allows me to think that I am writing my story, the truth is, I am not. And if I knew the whole story, if I knew what all the pieces were and how they fit and why they were important for the story to be uniquely mine, I would not act out the parts. There are parts I could never allow myself to say, to do, or to live through. No matter how important the part is to my life story, I still would not willingly act out that part nor follow the prompting of the director Himself. I trust Him, yes. I know God means me no harm. I know He is not sadistic or a cruel careless child. I know God is not insensitive. He knows what He is doing and why. But I still would not do it, my life, because I am not God. I am weak. I am a coward. I like being comfortable and having expectations and I long to be loved. Lord knows, my whole life is the story of my pursuit for love. I want to be loved by everyone. I think I embrace the stage, because up there, if you deliver the best music that comforts, inspires, and lifts others up to another world, they will love you. They will want you. They will pursue you. And I have always wanted that.

My life is a huge pursuit of love. As a little girl I dreamed of having twelve children and a husband that adored me, a music career with fans and an entourage that ate me up morning noon and night, and family and friends that admired me and held me in high regard. It was my life's goal, ultimately, to be loved by everyone. I wanted to be a good person; the best of persons. I believed I could do it myself and everyone would say "Wow, Michelle is awesome! I want to be just like her." I think this was the same for my mother.

As I stated earlier, my parents' beginnings were opposite to each other. It is surprising that they ever got together and married. Mom's story is like mine, where I am sure she would have been happier if God had given her a "how to" manual. My mother grew up in Brooklyn, New York, when the economy was booming and the streets in that area were safer than they are today. My grandfather was part of the black mafia, legend tells me. He was a boss. I cannot officially verify this, but I remember as a little girl witnessing large wads of money in his pockets or laying around on his bedroom dresser or the kitchen table as he ate his breakfast. There were various men that would come, and behind the large wooden sliding door that would separate his bedroom from the rest of his large bedroom upstairs, they would beg him for loans, for favors or, in some cases, for mercy. Grandpa was continually surrounded by silent men that stood ready to do what he wanted them to. Some came and left quickly to run some errand for my grandfather. There were many I saw that came once and never came back.

My grandparents wanted for nothing. Grandpa was a larger-than-life person standing over six feet tall with a large overshadowing form, decked out in three-piece suits and shiny leather shoes. His voice was large, loud, and commanding. My grandmother was small and thin, with long straight hair that she wore up most of the time. She was quiet with a soft voice. She could be stern when needed and had an unwavering faith in Jesus Christ. Grandpa had no such faith. His faith was in money. They lived in a brownstone, which was common for Brooklyn dwellers. Their home was on the basement and first floor level. Their furniture was leather, thick dark wood, and glass, nothing processed. Grandma had countless dishes and glassware, little knick-knacks worth a lot of pennies and memories, and clothes from Garfinckel's and Lord & Taylor. She never knew a Kmart.

Grandpa owned the house they lived in, so the tenants above them paid them the rent monthly. I knew of no one that crossed Grandpa in that brownstone nor paid the rent late except the one lady upstairs. She fussed and fumed about everything. But Grandpa never said anything to her or about her. She was one of Grandma's best friends. Grandpa smoked stinky cigars and drank bourbon. He smelled of the expensive stuff and heavy aftershave. My grandmother smelled of expensive perfume and wore a small amount of jewelry. Grandpa ran a furniture store and a moving company, which was probably a cover for whatever his real operations were.

My grandparents were proud people. Everyone knew them. They made sure Mom and Uncle Barney got the best education and a disciplined upbringing. Mom went on to college and studied world history and French. Uncle Barney joined the army. For a while, after college, Mom worked as a bank teller in Manhattan. She was super smart with numbers, and back then, it was not common for a black woman to hold such a job, so it said a lot about my mother. She was still 33 and living at home. Uncle Barney eventually married Aunt Carol. They had been together for a long time before they decided to get married. My mom did not seem to have any major aspirations for her life other than being a professor at a university. She planned one day to marry a young man that hung around her friend group. He wore fancy clothes he did not really have the money for and drove a fancy car he somehow obtained. Mom said he would throw money around like it was nothing, but he did not really have money like that. She liked him because he made her laugh and kept a smile on her face. Mom had a beautiful smile that made her large buck teeth light up a room. Her bright sparkling eyes and long slender legs were the talk of the town. My mother was a beauty, charming, and she did not know that about herself. Mom, Aunt Annalise, Vivian, Uncle Barney, and a few others would hang out after work and go to parties or to dances, then walk home along the streets laughing and enjoying their life.

Mom and Dad met at a bookstore. Dad was on furlough from the military for crimes of passion he had committed against a French woman while he was stationed there. He was waiting to answer for his "crime." Dad's story is very different from my mother's. My grandfather on my father's side came from Kashmir, India, before it was taken over by Pakistan after the Seventy-Year War. We were told he settled here in America with his wife, my grandmother, who was from Barbados. I do not know much about them. I never met them. I have only spoken to them over the phone. Grandpa was referred to as a blue-eyed devil. He was handsome, charming (the manipulative kind), and charismatic, and he knew he was a winner. He dressed sharply, smelled sharply, and believed himself to be the best. He loved to gamble, drink, womanize, and dance. He was far from being faithful to my grandmother. His straight wiry hair he wore slicked back, his olive complicated skin and his keen blue eyes from under his many hats made him the talk around town. They were dirt poor and always wanting. He would gamble for money then spend it on women and drink. So my dad knew all about hunger and not having enough to get by.

Grandma was a Holiness Baptist and believed she could pray the devil out of him. In their home she would hold all night prayer vigils with all the shouting and whooping and tongue-screaming that Holiness is known for. But Grandpa never changed his wicked ways. His photos screamed, "Ain't I pretty?", and he banked on it throughout his life. According to my father, Grandma may have prayed to God with great gusto for the salvation of her husband, but she lost all her sorrow within a bottle of alcohol nightly to forget the pain of her life. She stayed home and cared for my father and his two brothers, one younger and one older than him. She was a dark-skinned, barefoot, and rough-looking woman who knew all about woodstove backwoods hard work. They were poor, very poor.

Dad's education was spotty, and many times in life he had no shoes. Surrounded by a plethora of cousins, he had to fight for a scrap and the attention he so longed for. When he was 11, his oldest brother fell gravely ill with pneumonia. Back then there was no health insurance, especially if you were poor. People of color had to travel out of their way to get any medical care, and that was from a black doctor, if one could be found, with limited resources. So Grandma doctored him at home as best as she could, using home remedies from her beloved Barbados. But it was not enough. He died and her sorrow deepened further.

My dad was greatly affected by this loss and began to take on odd jobs around town to pay for things needed at home. Anything to be less poor was his goal. He delivered papers, did construction on plumbing, and ran electrical wiring, since he was small in stature. He delivered packages and worked on farms. He dutifully brought the money home to help his mom and his many siblings. His mother clung to his younger brother closely, never wanting him out of her sight. This caused jealousy between the brothers, as Dad felt neglected and resentful because he was trying to wear the shoes of the older brother and provide for his mom where his father had failed. Didn't anyone notice his effort? Why didn't anyone give him credit where he believed he deserved it? He tried desperately to save some of the money he made. He wanted to be a millionaire by a certain point in his life, but saving was next to impossible with all the needs back at home. His mother constantly reminded him he was just as much a blue-eyed devil as his father, and he would one day be just like him. Dad determined he would never be a loser like his father.

Around town, my father had a girlfriend, and they were constantly together. He planned to marry her one day, when he "made it." At some point Dad got her pregnant, and the whole family came down hard on him. To prove he was not like his father, he married her, and they set up house together. Dad worked hard to provide for her and his little girl. He was not even twenty yet when they got married. Things were very hard, and he was still providing for his mother and brother and helping with all the cousins. His mother's alcoholism was driving her to the grave, and it broke my father's heart. All she could see in Dad was her wayward husband and her dead son.

There was a day when my father was working, and his cousins and brother were going out on the town. Dad was supposed to go with them, but they decided to load up on the truck and not tell my father. As Dad saw them pulling out, he ran to catch them. They laughed and mocked Dad running after the pickup truck as fast as he could barefoot. He never caught them and was left at home.

I don't know what the event was that they were going to that was so important to my father, and I don't know why this event was so big to him, but after this, he packed a small bag of belongings and "ran away," as he said, from home. He did not like the way his life was going, and he could not bear to live under the scrutiny of his family and community anymore. He abandoned his young wife and daughter and joined the Army Air Force. While in line to be drafted, Dad changed his name. He took on the name Evan after the man standing in front of him and took on the name Moon after the man standing behind him and dropped his name "Khan" for the rest of his life. He was now Evan Moon. Dad was 16 when he enlisted. He believed, through the military, he would become a winner and find his life.

I do not know how or who or what, but at some point, Dad settled in Oklahoma with Sarah Anne. They had two children, Annabel and JoJo. Dad was serving in the military, and they lived decently in a nice home. Dad lied about his age and said he was 18. He thought he could go in and become an officer, but he had not finished school, and he was very rough around the edges, backwards, and country. The military in those days was extremely racist, and they did not give Dad an easy time. He was pretty like his father, with straight wiry hair and blue eyes. This set him apart from the other black men, as well as his charismatic charm and crafty ability to twist a word. But his country ways and accent made him fodder for ridicule.

While in the military, Dad completed his high school education, got a degree in metaphysics, and learned to drive a car. He also learned to drink, gamble, and womanize like his father. For a while Sarah Anne kept him straight. Dad wanted to fly the sky-scraping airplanes that were new to the military, but the furthest they were willing to put him was kitchen duty and cleanup. When

I was a little girl, my father would tell me stories of how he flew the different types of planes in the Air Force and what it was like to be up in the air. I really believed that is what my father did. When I became an adult, long after Dad died, I learned that he flew those planes from the ground in the kitchen preparing the men's meals.

Dad saw a lot of action while serving. When he was stationed in France, he met a French woman and fell in love. He got her pregnant with twins and thought he could forget about her by leaving back for the states. But European society is far different from American society. You get a woman pregnant; you are responsible to take care of her and the child. She pursued Dad through the military, then sent a special package home to Sarah Anne. It was a red fire truck with a letter. In the letter she told her how she had Dad's twin sons and he was responsible to take care of them. She sent a picture. Sarah Anne was devastated, and while Dad was at work, she packed her belongings and those of her two children, then left by taxi for the airport.

Somehow Dad learned of her leaving and raced home to chase the taxi down. He got there in time to watch his family board a plane and fly away to nowhere. Shortly thereafter, the military had him come in and he was charged. I do not recall what the charges or penalties were, and I do not know whether he lost pay or was demoted. I do know he was put on leave for a long time. This is how he ended up at the bookstore in New York where he and Mom met. Dad was drowning his sorrows of failure in alcohol and a "good time" in the big city. Mom was out on the town with her friends, hanging out on the weekend looking for a dance or party to go to, keeping in mind to be home before midnight. Grandpa was one to be reckoned with if she or Uncle Barney were even five minutes late. Even though Mom was 33, Grandpa would still swing the thick leather shaving strap known as Grandpa's belt if either of them got out of line.

When Mom met Dad that night, she thought she had died and gone to heaven. Dad was a dream in his military uniform, smelling of old spice and looking sharp with his devil's smile. Dad saw a naïve privileged little girl out looking for a good time. He thought it was his duty to help her have a good time. She invited him to join her and her friends. None of them liked Dad. There was something about him that they did not like, especially the gentleman that was sweet on my mom. They wanted Dad to go away, but Mom extended the invitation. He seemed like a lonely GI who just came back from fighting a terrible war and had no family to go home to. Shouldn't they give him a good time? Didn't he deserve it? He was in.

CHAPTER TWO

The Devil is In the Details

TRUCE(PICTURE OF BLUE FANTASY)

I DID NOT REALLY LISTEN
WHEN HE CAME AND ASKED ME TO COME HOME
I WAS LOST IN A HAZY VISION
SITTING ALL ALONE

I WANTED SO MUCH FROM LIFE
BUT IT NEVER WAS ALLOWED
MY SORROW OVERTOOK ME
I LOST THE WILL THE BOW

SOMETIMES TRYING DOES NOT WORK
AND LIFE COMES AND BEATS YOU DOWN
I AM BROKEN ON THE FLOOR
AND NO ONE IS AROUND

SOMETIMES CRYING DOES NOT HELP
I FILLED A GALLON WITH TEARS
THE MONSTERS ARE SALIVATING
HINGING ON MY FEARS

I CANNOT CONTROL THE TROUBLE
SCREWING UP MY BRAIN
I HAVE NO CONTROL OVER THIS
THE POWER TO BE SANE

I WANT TO GET IT TOGETHER
BUT I SLIDE INTO THE PIT
AND CHASE AWAY ALL OTHERS
WHEN MY MATCH IS LIT

I BROUGHT MYSELF TO HERE
BECAUSE ALONE I AM NOT SAFE
IT IS A TEMPORARY HAVEN
UNTIL I HAVE RELEASE DATE

BUT I FEAR MY FUTURE
MY BREAKS ARE MORE THAN FREQUENT
MY MIND WILL NOT STAY STILL
MY BACK IS NOW BENT

IF THERE IS A PLACE
I CAN CALL MY OWN
AWAY FROM ALL THE MASSES
ALLOWING PEACE AT LOAN

A PLACE WHERE I CAN STRETCH
AND PUT MY ART TO WORK
AND DANCE WITH ALL OF JOY
REWRITING MY LIFE'S BOOK

A PLACE WHERE MY MINDS TROUBLES
ARE NOT A POINT OF ATTACK
BUT EMPATHY IS MY PILLOW
AND LOVE I NEVER LACK

THEN I CAN PUT PLANS ASIDE
AND UNKNOT THE WAITING NOOSE
MOVE THE CHAIR TO ITS CORNER
AND GIVE DEATH ITS TRUCE

I have met the devil on several occasions throughout my life. He first introduced himself to me when I was a little baby. I have the distinct memory of a shadow at the foot of my crib and a black form of a man standing over me, watching me with piercing eyes. I did not like him, so I cried and then someone turned the light on to my room. I remember sensing something unwelcoming in the room and the hair on the back of my neck standing up. I knew instinctively he was not my friend. Why was he always staring at me, watching me? Why did he not go away? I hated when my mother put me down or my father would leave the room. I wanted them to stay and hold me, make me feel safe. But they were busy with other things, so I was put down and left alone in the crib or on the blanket on the floor. Then he would appear, stare at me, and watch me, and he would not go away.

When I was eleven months old, my mother's best friend took all of us in her 1968 Chrysler LeBaron to the emergency room at the hospital. Mom was screaming, holding her belly. What was in my mother's belly? She liked to talk to it a lot during the day, sometimes she would sing to her belly. I loved when my mother would sing to her belly. She used to sing to me, I remember. But now, she didn't do it anymore. All her focus was on her belly and my two older brothers. She was trying to teach them how to read, catch balls, and draw pictures. I would lay on my blanket and watch, wanting her to do the same with me. But right now, Mommy was screaming and crying big tears. I was sitting between her and Mrs. Betty, Mom's best friend. Mrs. Betty smelled like butter, cinnamon, and vanilla. I loved laying my head on her bosom. She was soft and pillowy. When I put my head on her, she would always smile. I liked making her smile, so I would lay my head on her and she would oblige.

Tonight, she was too busy consoling Mommy to notice me laying on her lap while she was driving. I almost went to sleep, but when we got to the emergency room, the door opened wide and the cold chilly winter wind blew in with lots of snowflakes. Nurses in white suits and hats helped my mother out of the car and into the building. Mrs. Betty parked the car right there with all of us kids huddling close up front. She turned on the Wi-Fi radio up loud to the "Quiet Storm" and we listened to the Commodores remind us that Christmas had just ended with Silent Night. "Come on kids, lets sing, okay?" Mrs. Betty encouraged nervously. I went to sleep.

When I awoke in my memories again, Daddy was dressing Brian in a small doll jacket and doll pants. Everything on him was so small, and everything on me was bigger now. My mother liked to make a lot of my dresses with matching hair bows. I was getting excited; today we were to go to the zoo. Daddy had talked about it all week with my brothers. I knew there were lots of animals there, very large ones. But I did not know what a zoo was yet. So it was exciting. I hoped Daddy would carry me the whole time we were there. Since Brian had been born, Daddy did not carry me as often. He had to carry Brian. Mommy was usually busy doing something with Cliff or Nathan. She would call me her good girl and would say she never had any trouble out of me, while I laid on my blanket or sat at my chair at the table. Then she would leave me to care for something with the boys or to change Brian's diaper. I wanted to say so much, but I had few words to use, and the ones I had did not seem to keep her with me or bring her back.

I liked to watch her and my brothers as they did things around the house or played outside while she hung the wash. My daddy would play with Brian once he got home from work in his pressed uniform and smile down at me. "There is our angel, never any trouble," he would say, and walk out the room playing astronaut with Brian. I liked to watch the sunlight dance on the floor in front of me or watch a bird on the windowsill looking in at me. I would hear the clock chime, the washer running, the music on the stereo playing, and I had nothing to say. I only listened and watched.

Sometimes in the corner of the room, the devil would sit and watch too. He would watch my family, my brothers, my parents doing the mashed potato to certain Motown songs. He would watch the neighbors come to our house in the evening and pick me up from my quiet corner to admire the handiwork of my mother's sewing and the softness of my person snuggling into whoever's bosom. He would watch the life of my family as intensely as I would watch from my clean sterile blanket corner, and he would not smile. He sat there darkly and watched.

I followed Daddy down the hall as he carried Brian in his arms towards the front door. He called for Cliff and Nathan to come join him. They obediently complied, putting on their shoes and snatching their jackets on their way out to the Chrysler Station wagon. Then Daddy put his large working black man's hand down into my face to stop my pursuit for the front door. "Hey, where are you going? This is for my boys and me, not you. I'm taking my men out with me to show them the zoo," he said proudly.

"Daddy," I pulled holding up my coat, but he took it away and handed it to my mommy. Then he gave her my hand and instructed her to not let me go out with them. I started to cry; I did not understand.

"See, I told you I never wanted any girls. They are too much trouble. I never wanted a girl," he gruffed and headed out the front door. I leaned against the screen with my tears smearing the netted metal, hoping he would turn around and change his mind and come pick me up and take me. But I watched him put my gleeful brothers into the car with him, turn the ignition and lights on, and pull the blue submarine out of the driveway and down our suburban street. I was completely crushed in my heart. What did Daddy mean, he never wanted a girl? I am a girl. He did not want me. Why? What did I do wrong? Why did he not want me? I looked up at my mommy, and she looked sad too. Does that mean Daddy did not want Mommy either? Mommy is a girl too, right? Why? Then I heard him. He never made a sound before, but today, he did. In the corner from us, the devil sat and laughed.

"Daddy I want to go. Please let me go too." I clung to his leg, but he pulled me off and shoved me away. He took Brian into his arms; he was about 15 months old. Nathan and Cliff ran out the door excitedly to the powdered blue 1969 station wagon parked in our weed-infested driveway. "I am only taking my boys. I never wanted a girl." he said looking down at me sternly. "The boys and I are going to the zoo." It's funny the things we remember when we are older. I remember plastering my face into the screen door and watching them pull out the driveway. My hot tears found no relief, and neither did my heart. Why did my daddy not want me? What did I do wrong? I was only about two-and-a-half, but it is one of my first memories.

Another first memory was when we went to Coney Island. We were on the beach with Grandma and Aunt Cocoa and my cousins. Mom was tired of holding me, so she sat me into the inflated tire and continued chatting to my aunt. The undertow snatched the tire and I started to float away from everyone, and no one noticed. I remember watching the people on the beach getting smaller and smaller until they were all like ants. Everything was very quiet save the call of seagulls and the water rocked me in the tire. I was not afraid. I remember I was not afraid, but

I wanted my mommy. I saw the lifeguard jump into the water. A few minutes later his funny face popped up out of the water and into mine and that scared me, so he started to play peek-a-boo with me and that made me laugh. He pulled me back to my mom and family and gave me to my mom. Everything went black after that; I don't recall what happened next. But I do remember that overall experience in my nightmares, and I wake up wondering, "Why did my mommy forget me?"

I used to daydream so much, my eyes were glued to a faraway horizon imagining queens and kings, princes and princesses, dragons and dukes, ladies in distress or Pocahontas running free in the virgin forest of the Americas. I would swing for hours outside on the swing set and sing to the top of my lungs some hymns Mommy taught me from church or songs I heard off the radio. If I got the tune wrong, I would start again and sing till I was on pitch perfectly and sang every note and every verse right like the singer who sang it. I sang those songs as if I understood what Diana Ross was saying or as if I was the one enticing the girl, like Nat King Cole. Other times I sat up in my tree for hours and watched the clouds quietly floating and the birds singing and chasing one another. But these things became my imaginary friends, and from that, an imaginary life of love and happiness that did not exist. I imagined my life like a big Hollywood movie, gorgeous and glamorous and full of families loving each other and warm chocolate chip cookies every night. Even through the choking smoke of my father stinky cigarettes, I conjured up "Leave It to Beaver" notions of my family that put a smile inside my heart and kept me innocent in my mind despite the reality that played out nightly before my young eyes and impressionable ears—Dad screaming hateful slurs at my mom, and my mother courageously defending herself and attempting to make my father put things in a right perspective.

These loud nights would end in my mother's woeful tears and a quick call to Grandma, who would put Grandpa on the phone, and he would chew my dad out for upsetting his daughter. Then the phone would hang up and Dad would pursue my mother from room to room apologizing until he hit on the right thing to say and the right words to use. This strategy of my mother's seemed to work well for her until the day my grandfather died. Then there were no more apologies; only angry ugliness, and eventual violence.

I loved how Michael Jackson sang his songs and phrased words from his thin invisible lips. He was my idol and my hope for the future. I dreamed of one day meeting the King of Pop and maybe, if I was lucky, performing with his majesty on the stage. It would have been magic. I believed he was my knight in shining armor, and if I was a good little girl and did everything right, Michael Jackson and the Jackson Five would one day come and deliver me from this terrible tower called my home, from the dragon called my dad, the wicked witch called my mom, and their three goblins called my brothers, and save me from an unimaginable fate of life without music. Yes, I could feel it, like the song says. They would come and rescue me and bring me to the kingdom of Carnegie Hall, where we would sing and celebrate the liberation of the world and love all over. No one would ever be hungry again, and no one would ever be without love. It would be perfect; mankind would be delivered from evil and would be a united family. This was my fantasy and my dream. Mom and Dad were not impressed by Michael Jackson. They liked Diana Ross, Gladys Knight and the Pips, Luther Vandross, Nat King Cole, Dinah Washington, Billie Holiday, and Frank Sinatra. Daddy wanted me to sing just like them; so did Grandpa. At family reunions, I would get the request to sing the Supremes, and I would get up and do my rendition of "Ain't No Mountain High Enough." Singing was the only time I would make my father smile. The only time I could feel my dad love me. Music was the love that seemed to unite us together.

I was not poor. Far be it from longing for shoes or a coat. I never wanted for these things. I never went once without food either. I always had more than I needed. I remember trips to the commissary where after shopping, my mom would stuff two wagons worth of groceries into the station wagon burying her four children underneath it all. And to keep us all quiet and uncomplaining, she would stuff our faces with cherry, lemon, or chocolate pies—treats for helping with the groceries and not complaining. Clothes were never an issue either. Commonly our clothes came from Woolworth's, or they were ordered from Garfinckel's in New York. There was a small boutique in our area where my mother took me for Sunday dresses and stockings. We were spoiled in the way of material goods. I went weekly to the beauty parlor to get my hair done once I turned eleven. Every night my mother brushed my hair out, greased it, and put it back up in braids—and later, curlers. Then I did her hair and rolled it up for her.

Mom doted on me physically. She washed me in the bathtub each night till I was twelve, spoon-fed me all my food till I was seven, and I read my mom my bedtime stories every night from the age of four until a teenager. During my teenage years I was made to recite famous speeches by heart from famous authors or sing a hard piece of music, whether Italian or German. If my mom did not buy the clothes, she sewed them. Mom loved sewing on her Sears sewing machine, and I was her model. She was a good seamstress and could have done this as work for a living. She made cute little green and red dresses, yellow and blue dresses, and she put big bows in my hair and stockings to match with little white sweaters and brown or black hush puppy shoes. I was a pretty child when my mother got done with me, smelling of baby oil and baby powder, and in my arms, I regularly carried a baby doll. This was my father's doing, baby dolls and coloring books. I had a bed covered in baby dolls and a stand of porcelain dolls of everyone from each country. I was so proud of my collection and would sit beneath the shelf tower staring at each one and imagining their lives.

Mom and Dad believed in education and made a point of making sure each one of us children were smart. We each learned to read around three years old. We started our education of spelling, phonics, mathematics, history, speech, and music around this time. We were Mom's little school before homeschooling became the vogue. Any schoolbooks Mom could get her hands on from substituting in the school system became part of our self-imposed education. Mom did not just teach us; she discussed the who, what, when, where, why, and how with us. If we had to experiment or experience something to understand it, Mom delivered the field trips or the science projects. She opened the curiosity inside our growing developing minds and taught us to think for ourselves.

When Daddy came home, he would review our work with us to see if we understood all we learned from Mom and later from school and Mom. If we got it right, we got praised, and if we got it wrong, he destroyed us. It was common to be called a jackass, dummy, stupid, ignorant, idiot, a waste of my time. I did not like my father's name calling. It hurt too much. I strove for perfection, and in return my dad was silent, withholding the praise I needed and longed for. I never knew if I was doing it right or well. And even when others would congratulate me, it never meant anything. I needed to hear my father tell me I did well. And he never did. It was only the last six months of my father's life that he finally said, "I love you and I am proud of you."

I hated being alone. It was common to find me living behind my father's chair with all my baby dolls circled around me and a blue blanket tied around my head playing Mother Mary. I would take another doll blanket and my sheets and create a tent and a nest within it behind my daddy's chair; there I would sit with eight dolls around me. I would scold them and correct them; then I would sing to them all the songs I had memorized inside my head, which were a lot. No one told me to be quiet, and many times Dad would turn the news down to listen to me singing. When I was a teenager and belting out "Gloria" from the radio as if it were my song, my dad would open my room door and stand in the door and listen without my knowing. He told me about how he would be drawn to my singing when he was months away from dying. It was what led him to sending me to music camp when I entered seventh grade. My precociousness paid off, and music camp developed all that raw uncontrollable music energy and unrealistic imagination and taught me to take the words and the notes and to put them on paper. What good were the fantasies if they stayed inside my head? They could come out on a tape recorder or in a notebook on paper, and in this way, come to life.

Being surrounded by all that music, the voices, and the instruments all day long, thinking about clef notes and grand staffs and arpeggios, it was a dream. An unimaginable dream that went on and on. Once back home to my life, I learned to take the notes and transform them into words—rhyming words. Soon poetry and prose were my thing. I might not speak in school, but my poetry spoke volumes. I finally had a voice, and my teachers were sitting up and listening. One teacher in the seventh grade wised up and figured out how to get me to talk in school. He asked me to read from the textbook, which I willingly did. Suddenly I had a voice. That "little girl" voice no one knew came out and made the words on the page jump out.

My English teacher got with Mrs. Random—she was the speech teacher—and asked my parents to meet with me after school. She gave me a piece of poetry to read by Edgar Allan Poe called "The Raven," and without any coaching from either of them, I read it with great passion. I understood what Mr. Poe was trying to relate, and like singing a song, I could convey those thoughts in my reading. Reading and writing became the catalyst into a new world of speech for me.

After Grandpa had died, life began to change. Before there were threats of violence and abandonment. After Grandpa was gone, Dad made good on his threats. Dad began to drink far more than before and did not hide his liberation around us. He was mean. He did not hold back from cursing us children out in a heartbeat. We could do no right, no matter how much we tried. We were dumb, ignorant children, and we needed a good beating to knock the sense into us. It was like being whipped like a slave. He would line us up against the wall and go down the line whipping legs, arms, hips, thighs, anything exposed and not exposed. He would whip us until we had black and blue marks, and we cried a river none ending. I learned to escape into my head so that I could not feel the sting and the pitiful cries of my brothers beside me. If one of us messed up, we all got a whooping. Mom could not take these severe corporal punishments, so she would volunteer to do the whoopings. She was not much better, but at least we would not be lined up against the wall, and at least we were not demeaned and called "stupid" and "jackass." Over Mommy's knee we would go, and down would come the leather strap good and hard. I do not recall my mother leaving bruises on me, but I do recall not being able to sit down for a while without being very sore.

Daddy never hit or beat my mom, only my brothers and me. Despite how he hurt my mother constantly, I truly believe he loved her up to the day she died. But I do not think we children were what he wanted, especially me, and he took all his anger and wrath out on us, especially my brother Nathan, who was autistic. To my dad, Nathan was stupid, and cruelty would help him find his intelligence. I could not stand how my father treated him, and many times I would lie and take the blame for Nathan's offenses so I could receive his discipline. There was no sound I hated more than Nathan's pitiful soul-wrenching cries when my father would slap him down to the ground for forgetting how to set the table, or for sneezing without covering his mouth, or worse, for making a funny comment about bathroom experiences. Nathan had the sweetest disposition for a boy. He was one of those children you just wanted to scoop up into your arms and hold and love on. Even as a teenager, he was not considered very handsome, but his personality was soft and gentle, the kind a girl felt safe around and would feel she could confide in, and that is what many of the girls in school would do. Dad saw this as a weakness and regularly beat my brother to knock it out of him. He saw it as toughing him up.

Nathan was another one of us that was quiet and not popular like my other two brothers. He had buck teeth like myself, only his stuck all the way out, and he could not close his mouth, so like me, he had a full mouth of braces and a retainer. He wore large-rimmed thick glasses, and he did not hold back from reciting one of his lists, whether it was all the streets in Dale City or the top 100 artists on the radio; Nathan was a brainiac with a photographic memory. Yet he was stuck going to the "special school" for "special kids" on the "short bus." He was autistic with Asperger's syndrome, but my parents were in awful denial of the truth. Nathan was constantly picked on by the kids at my school and in our community, as well as Dad.

Once as a joke my dad told us all he was moving us a block away from our home to another house: Garfinkle High School territory. We were absolutely petrified, and for thirty days all of us were in intense panic. The kids in that school deeply hated us, because my dad had arrested so many of the kids that went there. They threatened to kill us if we ever went to their school. We pleaded nightly for our father not to move us there. He got a kick out of watching us stress over the possible move. He even put a "for sale" sign out increasing our panic. Eventually he took the sign down and told us he was just kidding. He wanted to see what our reaction would be.

Nathan suffered the most from that situation. At one point he stood on the banister of the back porch and threatened to jump and kill himself. He could not take it anymore. At the time, as kids, we thought he could really kill himself, but now, as an adult, the most damage he might have done was maybe break his ankle or something. But we did not know. It was Nathan's first threat of suicide.

We were going out of our way to defend him, especially me at home before my dad. Once the neighborhood bully, Marley, tried to beat Nathan up and threw an ice ball at him, hitting him in the head. My three brothers later came out of the house and marched down to Marley's house to confront him for hurting our brother and at the bus stop. His parents made him march back to our house and apologize personally to Nathan so that my brothers did not fulfill their threat of beating Marley up for what he did. Another time, Cliff, as usual, was invited to someone's house party. Nathan wanted to go but the kids laughed at him to think he would go to their party. Angry, Cliff took the time to dress his brother up and take him with him to the party, using the excuse that our parents wanted Nathan to chaperone him and make sure he stayed out of trouble.

As kids we were kind of close to one another, and we would defend each other at school and at home. Mr. *NOBODY* had a permanent residence in our home, so did Mr. *I DON'T KNOW*. It would burn my parents up, but we had each other's back most of the time, especially Nathan's. We'd rather protect each other than live through the blood-curdling screams of someone getting mercilessly whipped by my dad, or worse, punched or slapped. And none of us wanted to watch my mother spank us in place of Dad because Dad forced her to do so. That just tore us up the worst, even though she spanked us with all the fervor of conviction of believing we deserved it.

Nathan and I both shared a passion for music, but on different instruments. I played the piano wanting to be like Stevie Wonder, and Nathan played the violin, but he could play anything he heard on the radio by ear. I was glued to the music in front of me. Cliff also had a passion for music, playing his alto saxophone day and night. Like Nathan, he could play anything heard on the radio and read music. Brian was the only one of us four that never settled on any instrument. All of us could also sing; I was usually the lead singer and they would be my "Pips." We would pretend to be a music band complete with our instruments and dance moves taught to us by Cliff like the Jackson 5. They never really took any of this play seriously, but I did. I wanted us to be a famous group of some kind. I was rehearsing for taking the world by storm. I dreamed of going to the Apollo. That was never their dream.

We would listen to Quiet Storm in the basement before dinner and play along with whatever came on. My father later bought me a keyboard so I could play piano in my room or in the basement, instead of in the living room on the real piano where his news would be interrupted. Some songs we would do repeatedly by playing tape cassettes of recorded music. Other times Cliff and I would practice our dance moves in the evenings, learning how to hustle, moonwalk, and dance like James Brown. We both got pretty good and made a good team, but again, it was always my dream and not his. But at that age, I never really knew it. On Saturdays our favorite program, Soul Train, came on, and we all prepared to sing and dance with whoever came on. We tried our best to be on our best behavior so that we would not miss Soul Train. We learned most of our dance moves off of Soul Train. There was also the Solid Gold dancers and Casey Kasem's program too. These were some of our greatest idols and a form of escape. But the height of my escape was the program *Fame.*

I was lost in the program *Fame.* Irene Cara was me, and her boyfriend was my future boyfriend. The story line was my future. This was my life. It made a huge impression on me. To make it, I needed to know how to dance, speak, sing, and act. I taught myself and I set my mind on just that. I spent six hours or more a day whenever I could play the piano and spent that same amount of time practicing singing. My mother had me rehearse in the evening on my speech and poise. She and my grandmother also had their heart set on me becoming an accomplished musician, but for different reasons. They both felt I would make a very good teacher or a professor in some college of music, and so they groomed me towards that. When I turned thirteen, my mother sent me to auditions at the Duke Ellington School of Performing Arts in Washington, DC. I was a pretty good artist, too, and begged my mother to let me try out in art as well as music. She relented and allowed it, and I was accepted into the school on both accounts.

My father did not want me to go because the school was in DC, so for six weeks, I went to the school of my dreams without my father knowing. I was living *FAME*, the program, and it was the happiest time of my life. I was surrounded by others just like me who had large dreams and who were just as highly intelligent. By then I was speaking in school, though very shy. But here, I was a regular chatterbox, and I made friends quickly. No one cared for my looks. I was not Fea; all that was important was learning ballet and tap steps, getting the arpeggios down, and memorizing the music and words to the plays we had to perform, as well as studying ferociously to keep our C+ average or higher. The challenges were welcomed and exhilarating. My home life meant nothing to me, and I did not have the extra load of cruel kids at school. Plus the combined secret between me, my mom, and Grandma was a lot of fun.

"This is what your grandfather wanted for you," Grandma said. "He would have paid for this, but you made it happen."

They were proud of me and I felt good. But my balloon popped when it was open house night for the parents, and my father got the phone call before my mother did. He was hot, but he willingly went to the open house to see for himself what I had been learning and doing. Everything impressed him that evening, and I was certain I was a shoo-in with my dad till he met one of my friends. I do not remember his name, but he was blatantly and flaming gay, and he was not eighteen yet. He came over in a pink bodysuit and introduced himself to my father in his soft, sensitive way. My father was appalled and would not shake his hand. I giggled because his behavior I found to be funny. I did not know what it meant to be gay yet. After the introduction, driving home, my father refused to allow me to return, and I cried bitterly that night for hours. The next week I was enrolled into Woodbridge Middle School. I would try out again the following year to go there for high school. Again, I was accepted for my singing, and this time my father said no and made sure I showed up for the first day of school at Osbourn Park High School. I never forgave him at that time for crushing my dreams.

My mother wanted me to make it big, but she wanted me to do it her way. A neighbor in the community started a community choir, and my mother supported all of us kids joining. I was the only one to join. I knew Mrs. Blue's daughters very well. We knew each other and had played together since the third grade. They called me names too and excluded me from play sometimes, but they were not as mean to me as others. Their mother knew Jesus personally, and she made it her business to make sure the rest of us would too, especially me and my brothers.

It was not unknown in our community that my father was a Muslim by faith and in practice, and he had a deep hatred towards anything Christian. He went out of his way to defame anyone who spoke openly about Christ, and as Captain over at Lorton, he made it extremely difficult for any minister to have a prison ministry. If he did not like you, Dad would find reason to dig up dirt on you and cause you to lose your job, get arrested, or worse, lose your clerical collar. Dad despised Christians. There were ministers in our community who tried to get through to my dad and befriend him, but they always got a slammed door in their face and later a heartfelt apology from my mom. Only two were able to break my father's black ice: Reverend Jones and Pastor Holy. Pastor Holy eventually would spend most of his time ministering to my mom and us kids when he paid his monthly visits, but it was Reverend Jones my dad would have inside the house and at the table for coffee, chit chat, and laughs.

Our mother made us go to the local Lutheran church that Pastor Holy led after I made a comment to my grandmother one evening while she was doing my hair that I did not know who was in the picture on her dresser. Of course, it was Jesus praying in the Garden of Gethsemane (my grandmother had a strong Christian faith), but it was very upsetting to her that I did not know who Jesus was. Afterwards, we all received red Bibles and were quickly baptized (sprinkled) with water in the church. Mrs. Blue befriended my mom later and asked if we children would join her little mission choir. I joined, hoping for the opportunity to demonstrate my singing abilities, not because I believed in Jesus. In fact, at that time, age twelve, I believed in God, but not Jesus. But I kept that fact to myself for a while.

The first night of choir practice we went over various songs that everyone seemed to know but me. Where I was traditionally hymn songs and could sing any one of them from the heart, everyone else seemed traditionally Pentecostal and sang upbeat worship songs following Mrs. Blue's records that, to me, had a lot of Motown and Ray Charles rhythms in them. It was surprising but also very appealing. Much of it was Shirley Caesar's, but I did not know at the time. I was quickly chosen by the choir to lead the songs, and everyone else would back me up. For the men's parts, they kept talking about Donny and Immanuel Blowfish.

"Who are they?" I asked. I wondered who they were and why they were not here yet.

"Wait and see," Samantha and Shirley warned. "They are coming, but only after choir is over. They are always late, and they are not like any guys you ever met."

"What do you mean?" I asked.

The girls laughed at the fact that I never heard of the infamous Blowfish boys. There were seven of them, but Johnny did not live with them at the time. They all wore polyester suits and black roach killer shoes and carried large King James Bibles in their hands like good Pentecostals. They all could pray in tongues down to Darnell, the youngest; they all could be slain in the spirit on cue and could pray out loud, loud enough to scare the devil away. Oh, I was in for a treat. So after choir practice was over and most of the choir had left for home, I waited two hours past just to get a glimpse of these Blowfish boys. As promised, the older ones were dressed in three-piece polyester suits and ties with roach killer shoes. They all looked like traveling salesmen right down to their dad. They all had similar bashful smiles except for Immanuel.

There was nothing bashful about Immanuel. He was very authoritarian and confident like an adult, and that scared me. While we prayed with their parents, Samantha made a side comment about how funny Mrs. Blowfish's prayer sounded, and of course, we giggled with our hands over our mouths. When prayer was over, Immanuel ripped into us, equipped with scripture, about how children ought to respect and honor their parents and the authorities over them, and suggested that our behavior was as sinful as if we had killed someone, and we needed to repent now. My first impression was that he was handsome but too frightening for me to give any interest.

My interest, like so many of us in the choir, fell on Donny, the rebel, whom we later named Superfly. He was in a three-piece like his brothers, but he was far from looking like a traveling salesman. He looked more like Prince Charming, wearing a red cummerbund and bow tie to complete his black suits, instead of the usual tie and grey or brown suit like his brothers. His hair was slicked back and straight with slight curls (he later colored it brown and grew it long like a white boy, over his eye). His eyes were confidant and mesmerizing. I do not think he had any idea how many of us girls dreamed of being his girlfriend, and I am sure I do not know how many of us got the honor. I just know I was not one of them. Nevertheless, Mrs. Blue and the choir had other plans for me.

Out of all the Blowfish boys, there was one who was similar in character to me—Jacob. He was not just bashful, quietly looking down at his feet with a goofy smile written over his face. He too was very shy and overly intelligent, not just in scripture but also academically. He sat away from the others like me. Both of us had strong voices, so the choir voted for Jacob to be the vice president and me to be the president as a joke. How could both us lead when we were both too afraid to open our mouths and talk, let alone look up at anyone? We had to exchange phone numbers. After I got home, around 11 p.m., Jacob called me on the kitchen phone, and we talked for hours into the night. This would be the first of many nightly and daily phone calls between the two of us. And we both surprised our choir mates by demonstrating how much we were natural-born leaders and made a well-oiled machine when we worked together.

Once we got some of the music down pat and complimentary costumes to wear, Mrs. Blue took us on tour to various Pentecostal churches. We were good, and we brought many to tears, or, in their fervor, to being "slain in the spirit." At one point we were getting popular. I look back and wonder how I could sing so expressively words I had no understanding of, but I thought I had made it. I thought if I kept it up and sang with all my heart I would be discovered. I would one day make it, I believed, so I did the circuit with the group, singing my heart out to Jesus and dreaming of being a star.

I was popular in school for the wrong reasons and for the right reasons. I was famous academically for my high intelligence among the teachers, so much so that in many of my classes the teachers would ask me not to answer all the questions, and to give the other kids a chance. So that I did not grow bored, many of my teachers gave me extra credit work, which I gladly enjoyed doing. I loved schoolwork; it was another form of escape. Some groups of kids would regularly haunt me during lunch, wanting me to do their homework or they would beat me up. I would take my glasses off and tell them to do their worst. They did, but I would not do their homework. Other times my homework would be stolen while in the locker room or in the bathroom. Like Nathan, I had a photographic memory, and it was not hard to rewrite very quickly my homework or a paper due before I had to hand it in.

It was easy to make A's in class, except for math, and later some of my science classes. I was also very popular for my singing, for being on the debate team, and for forensicating. By my high school years, I was a power to be reckoned with. It was common for us to bring home first place. But if by chance, we got second place, we worked hard to go from second place back to first place. I was viciously competitive, and showed no mercy to anyone I competed with, because I focused on only getting my father's approval. On my debate team, I was known as the tiger. My other partners would start the debate out, and when we got to the end, I was sent in for the kill, and kill I would. I wanted my father's approval. I never got it. Once I won a trophy as tall as myself and brought it home, proud and sure my father would say those magic words, "I love you." But he never did. Instead, he donated my trophy back to the school for their showcase instead of keeping it in our home. For many years, I could not forgive him for that. He never told me whether he was proud of my winning or not.

Art was another area I excelled and competed in, as well as my poetry and prose. Once I offered my cartoon skit to the Potomac News. They offered me a job as a writer until they learned my age, thirteen. "Come back to us when you graduate from high school," they encouraged me. Another competition I entered, I won all-school and later all-county for my poetry, and I was in seventh grade. I surprised my community at how gifted I was. The only one that said nothing and showed no emotion was my dad. This had always hurt me. Even in my piano recitals, I would practice with great intensity to get it right. But one recital when I was twelve, I was playing the blue Danube and I forgot my notes. I sat in silence for what seemed ages until I could remember my part again. This, my father criticized me for, and after that, he never came to another one of my recitals again.

But I was also popular for the wrong reasons. Mom was strong-willed and stubborn as a mule. My dad may have refused to say anything of my gifts, but not my mother; she had her mind set as to what she wanted for my future and which way I was going. The more wins I had, the more my mother made me work. Free time outside at the creek or in the woods, and playing handball or kickball with the kids were things of the past once I turned fourteen. It was piano, dance, speech, poise, reading, etiquette, memorizing, and later, learning to be a lady, as my mother prepared me to be a debutante.

My ugliness, according to my peers, made me popular. By now I had thick untamed hair I still wore like a little girl even up to the age of sixteen. I had thin legs, thin arms, a bump for a butt, and bumps for tits, but the biggest thing on me besides my teeth were my glasses and the mountain of pimples across my forehead. My mother worked tirelessly with medication from the doctor to heal the black and brown pimples that dotted my face and nose. Nightly we scrubbed my face till the pimples bled trying to make them disappear. She would lather Noxzema on my face, and I went to bed at night with the white mask on. Finally, mother hid them under thick bangs. It helped give my face some improvement, but the kids still called me ugly.

Another shortcoming was the invading rash of atopic eczema. It enveloped my face, scalp, arms, legs, and chest, but especially my hands. It made my skin look scaly like a lizard, and I hated wearing short sleeves or shorts because the kids could see it, so I avoided clothing that exposed it, no matter how hot the day. It was common for me to wear long-sleeved sweaters over the summer. My mom would have me wash my hands excessively as if the eczema could be washed off. At night she scrubbed me thoroughly trying to make the eczema go away. Then she would cover me up with calamine lotion, with long socks on my feet and gloves on my hands so I would not scratch. But the eczema would not go away. The kids taunted me so ruthlessly because of my hands; then my mother got the bright idea of buying me multicolored gloves to wear on my hands covering the eczema. I thought I looked like Michael Jackson, only I wore gloves on both hands instead of one, like him. My gloves made me feel safe and very special. I wore them throughout high school.

Mother and I fought tirelessly as our dreams for my life were similar but divided. I wanted to be a performer; she wanted me to be a teacher. She trained my voice to be operatic, though I wanted to sing the blues like Billie Holiday. When I practiced my secular music, she would yell down the hall for me to pull out my Italian arias and practice what her money was paying for. When I would play music by the Commodores on the piano, she would close the book and say "Enough of that; now practice Chopin for me for about an hour." And I would, resentfully. By high school, in retaliation towards my mother insisting that I play classical music versus my contemporary loves, I refused to go to piano practice. "Fine," Dad said, "I can save my money and not send you anymore." I later found someone else in the community to give me lessons. I wanted to learn to play by ear, but she was not as good or attentive a teacher as my original, and I became discouraged and practiced less.

Later, Mr. Grain from Dale City Christian Church became my voice and piano teacher. He was a tall, thin, energetic, and talkative man; a musical genius, strung out on cocaine. He continued my classical lessons in voice and piano to my own chagrin, but he also taught me stage presence, professionalism, and perfectionism. He would practice me in voice and piano at the church till he had me in tears. Practice was never over until I got it right, even if he just gave me the piece that day. By seventeen I was an accomplished musician with a large repertoire of classical, contemporary, and show tune music that I could either play on the piano reading music or sing at the drop of a hat by heart.

With my dream of becoming a famous singer, I also dreamed of escaping from my loveless home life and becoming a mother and a housewife. I know that this observation is scathing of my family and I don't mean it to be this way, but at the time, no one in our house said "I love you" to each other; no one gave or received hugs or said things like "I'm proud of you." It was expected that you would make A's or get whooped. You would excel in whatever you were made to do or get whooped. You could not fail; that was understood. It was also understood that whatever demons lived in our house, we were to keep in our house and between us only. There were many demons in our house, and most of them resided in my father.

When I was still a child, my father would drink alcohol and get drunk at night while watching his late shows and westerns on TV. He would argue and fight with my mother, demeaning her and putting her down. In the evenings, if he were home from work, he would choose the child to pick on for the night, and rip into that one till that child was nothing but a nub. There never was a reason; he had to pick on someone. We would hide out in our rooms and hope he would not choose us, or hide in the basement in front of the TV watching the Muppets or the new stolen cable HBO (without our parents' knowledge) or even MTV again without their knowledge, hoping and praying he would forget we existed. Just one night, but that one night never came. Once he was done ripping into you and exposing all your weaknesses and faults, even laughing at your failures and mistakes, he would send you away ashamed and humiliated. Don't dare think to cry, that resulted in a slap or a punch for my brothers (as an adult, once I moved away, I had to teach myself how to cry again because I got good at holding it all in) or a slap for myself. And if you had the audacity to fight back or argue back, as Cliff and I regularly made the mistake of doing, he did not hesitate to slap you down or hit you till you begged him off.

If Nathan's name got called, one of us would do something stupid to get his attention off Nathan and onto someone else so that Nathan could be spared. No one ever liked watching Dad tear Nathan apart.

The most hideous demon living in our house that stayed a family secret was my father's relationship to me. And I am assuming I am the only one, because none of my brothers ever admitted to experiencing being made to play horse with Dad. The devil lived in my house, and his name was Daddy. It started when I was five, as far as I remember, and playing alone in the family room with my Barbies. My father came down and came from behind me. I thought he was going to hug me, and it made me so happy to feel his arms around me because it was rare. But I felt his hands down there and sensations that were foreign and I did not understand. It happened a few other times and I said nothing. I liked the fact that at least my father was showing affection for me. Brian accidently walked in and saw once. He told my mom it was my brother and she scolded him for doing it instead of my father. Later it stopped happening during the day and he would come visit me at night after my brother Brian moved out of my room, being too old to sleep in the bed next to me. He would come home from work and I would hear the car door slam, hear him march up the concrete steps outside and put the jingling keys in the door lock, then slam the front door. His shoes would clip down the hall till his shadow stood in my doorway. He would come in my room, close the door, sit beside my bed, and play with me. I watched him silently, feeling the sensations and saying nothing. I laid there and looked at my father's face, happy to get attention even if I did not understand what he was doing. It made me feel funny and I did not like that, but I wanted my daddy to want me and if this were how he could want me, then in my child's mind, it was okay. He did this to me till puberty hit and things changed.

When he stood in my doorway, he told me to go and sit on the couch in the living room and wait for him. I did obediently. He would change his clothes, then go in the kitchen and pour his Jack Daniels and Kool Aid or Jack Daniels and orange juice in two separate 7-Eleven moose cups, as well as a cup of steaming hot black coffee. He would come sit in his lounge chair across from me on the couch, then turn on his late shows. He would chug down one of the cups, sip his coffee, take a smoke of his pall malls, then move to the edge of his seat, look me squarely in the eyes, and threaten to do me bodily harm if I moved, opened my mouth, or even fell asleep. I was to give him all my attention. He would say "Is that clear?" I would respond with "Yes sir." He would then proceed to tell me why my mother was a failure of a wife; why all of us kids would live to be unsuccessful, except for Brian, my baby brother; and why he hated my grandfather. He would then tell me in detail about the inmates at the prison and what they did to get there. He would tell me how he decimated another preacher and kept him from coming in the jail or how he arrested another one of Cliff's friends and how Cliff would end up just like them. He told me about the war and all he lived through, people dying, being blown up, or shot away.

I relived every awful memory and experience my father ever lived through as if I went to Vietnam, as if my father left me and my mother threw me out and made me homeless at sixteen. I was about twelve when he started this ritual. It was a Saturday afternoon and it would go on into the early morning hours before he drifted off into a drunken sleep and I was free to carefully climb over him and back into my bed. I do not remember whether he continued playing horse with me or whether, because of trauma, I erased it from my memory. But the nightly rituals with him paved the foundation for my eventual crippling agoraphobia in adulthood and distaste and shame for anything sexual. This continued with my dad till the night I married.

Despite battling with my father's constant demons, I wanted to have twelve children and be like the Brady Bunch or a rendition of the Cosby family. I had picked out names for each of my children, and I prayed over all of them every night.

My firstborn would be Sarah Abigail; then there would be Joshua and Josiah the twins; then Rebecca, Suzannah, Gladys, Benjamin, Joseph, Daniel, Elizabeth, Julianne, and David. I truly believed I would have twelve children, but what of a husband? I was too ugly for any of the boys in school. No one wanted me, but I had a few in mind. For me it was a tossup between Roberto Torricelli and Donny Blowfish. Originally, I made Immanuel Blowfish my first choice, but that first meeting and his burning anger and rebuke over our teasing his mom cooled any crush I might have had. Jacob was a name that the girls in the choir would hound me with, but I was not originally interested. He was too much like a big brother to be a choice for a husband. Besides, Roberto's name conjured up romantic notions like in the movies.

Roberto had curly dark brown hair and round satin brown eyes; he wore a wiley smile and was highly intelligent like me. Once in the lunchroom we got into a debate on a random subject. My voice apparently got loud so he got louder. So I got louder than him. Not to be outdone, he stood on his chair continuing our debate, so I stood on mine and we were nose-to-nose. He suddenly went quiet and looked around us. everyone in the cafeteria had gone quiet listening to us go at it. I tried to get down off my chair feeling embarrassed, but he took my arm and kept me there. Well done, he said, and we got down off our chairs together. The cafeteria applauded us. His eyes had turned green with the intensity of our debate, and I shivered with a schoolgirls undying crush. That night I wrote a love letter to my hopeful future husband with a poem, and climbing the stairs the next day headed for class, slipped it into his hands as I passed him by. It was the boldest thing I had known myself to do to date. Later, a few days later, he confronted me with, "I like you as a good friend, a best friend, could we just be that?"

Hopes of matrimony to my prince died after that. But hopes for Donny still survived for a while. I was raised to believe marriage was a woman's ultimate fulfillment and expectation, and that marriage occurred shortly after graduating from high school, if not before. And so I pursued that false belief, even though no one else was following that for me.

Another consideration was my cousin Francis. He was not my true cousin, but we all grew up together since diapers. Aunt Amy was my mother's best friend from New York. I loved her and my cousins dearly, and from the time that I was seven we would spend each summer in New York, first at Grandma's house, then Aunt Carol's house, then later Aunt Amy's house. Bobby and Francis were like brothers to me. Coco and Lilly were like my sisters more than cousins as well. We all spent so much time together in sizzling New York summers.

When I was four-and-a-half years old, Bobby and I were coloring out on the porch together till it was time to come in and take a nap. We were about the same age. It was a sweaty summer, and I quickly dozed off to sleep on top of my bed with the fan blowing. When I woke up, it was dark in the bedroom, so I got scared. I thought it was nighttime and everyone left me alone. Bobby was not on the other bed. I looked out my bedroom door and saw an orange light, so I decided to follow it down the hallway. When I got to the source, I stood spellbound staring at my kitchen on fire. I could not move; it was like I was glued looking at the flames licking up the side walls and onto the ceiling above me. It was like a dream until I saw the face of the monster (the fireman) staring down at me. I screamed and he picked me up, put something over my face, and carried me out. Outside it was still the afternoon. It is all I remember of that time, but I never got over my fear of fire.

A little while after that happened, Bobby was riding home from school in the car with his mom when their car was hit by another. Bobby's neck was snapped, and he died instantly. We got the call in the evening that Bobby had died, and Mom cried loudly as if she were in pain. I did not understand why she was crying and what she meant by saying Bobby was dead. At the funeral, everyone I loved was crying except me. I was smiling and going around hugging everyone. My Aunt Doris Lee made the comment that there was something wrong with me because I was so happy. It was not proper for a child to be so happy at a funeral. So Mom and Grandma walked me up to the casket to say goodbye to Bobby. I remember he was purple with a grimace on his face. He did not look like Bobby. He looked like a cartoon character and I laughed again. Mommy quickly rushed me away. In the funeral car sitting up front in between my parents, I turned around and looked at my relatives who were squeezed into the back seat and asked them why they were crying; we would see Bobby again. Then I turned around and hummed a song to myself. I don't know why I said that, but for years after I imagined Bobby had gone away on a journey, and if I waited long enough he would come back as my husband and take me away from Dale City, Virginia, to where we would live forever in Jamaica Queens, New York. As I got older and understood what death really was, my desire for Bobby to be my husband changed to Francis.

Francis was extremely handsome in a New York Italian way. His city accent left me spellbound, and I always felt so safe around him when we went sightseeing in New York City. He was gentle, kind, and understanding, and very much a big brother to me. In fact, too much of a big brother, and thoughts of marriage soon fizzled as well. My hero came in a different form, but it would be years before he was revealed to me; instead the one person I least expected decided he would become my future husband—Jacob.

CHAPTER THREE

A Way of Escape

There seemed to always be a void in my life. Something was missing, and I was always in search for that missing thing. The hole in my life was so large, and I was starving for something to fill it, but what?

God, are you there? God, do you love me? Do you see me? Am I important to you? Why am I here? Why does my father hate me so much? Why does my mother cry so much? Will I grow up to be very important? I want to leave, God. I want to get away from my father. He will not leave me alone, and I do not want to see him hurt my brothers anymore. How do we make him stop? Why are the kids at school so mean? I do not want to go to school anymore, God. God, why do you hate me so much? What did I do to make you hate me? I try so hard to be good, but I always mess up. Jacob and his brothers say you are a loving father and a good God. That you hear us when we pray and that you will give us good gifts if we ask. Well, I am asking, please get me away from my father. Please provide me a safe place to call home where people will love me, and I can love them back. Could you do this, and it will show me you are what they said. Amen.

Jacob and I would talk for hours unending on the phone as soon as we got home from school. On the weekends he would come to my house and spend all day there. We would spend hours jabbering away in the basement about everything and get into heated discussions or play board games where both of our competitive natures would come out and devour each other. The topic we argued about the most was faith. He was the Christian, and I was the agnostic on the verge of atheism being groomed by my father to become a proper Muslim woman and an Eastern Star. I had so much confusion caught up inside my head on the various topics, but I debated theology as if I were an authority on the subject. I wanted my questions answered, but most importantly to me at the time, I wanted to win every debate at all costs, and I wanted to prove that there was not a loving God, only a sadistic one out to destroy each of us, one by one. And that is how my silent observer, Lucifer, began to mold in my mind how cursed I was.

Sometimes Jacob's other brothers, Immanuel and Donny, would come over as well in Immanuel's beat-up pickup truck or dirty, noisy white van, and there we would go at it for hours in the basement debating theology and politics (something I was better versed on at the time). They passionately tried to convert me each time, and I just as passionately tried to stump them. You cannot convert someone who was cursed for life. My father did not want me because I was no good, useless. Why waste your breath? But you cannot say things like that in polite company. I learned that from my mom. It's improper to make someone feel sorry for you, even if it is one of the Blowfish boys. So you say nice things to make others feel better. I would deflect when it got personal. It was easier to talk about how hateful God is against their argument of how loving he is. Once my brother skipped school and got a Jheri curl. He looked good like one of the guys from Kool and the Gang. But we all knew Dad was not going to like it. He successfully dodged Dad until dinnertime. My father hit the roof. Dad screamed every description of sissy at Cliff, short of cussing, then dragged him by the neck to his room to sheer the beautiful curls off him. Tell me how God is loving when my father is so cruel.

Other times, as I got to know them better, Jacob's mom and dad allowed me to go over to their house. The first time I went over there, I was floored by the amount of clutter, furniture, boxes and personal belongings they had stored on their porch and flowing into the hall, living room, dining room, bedrooms, and especially the kitchen and bathrooms. There was no place to sit or even to use the toilet. The house was stuffed with boxes full of everything and anything. I could not see the floor, for we walked over papers and books and clothes. It was awful. My mother's house looked like a stark museum in comparison. And the smell was like extremely sweet food throughout the house. Once I cleared a spot on the couch, I was introduced to a colony of roaches creeping away from the exposure. So I learned to stand while I visited or to sit in a kitchen chair after wiping it off. Because of certain habits my mother instilled in me, other times I would begin to "clean their house" without being asked, starting in the room that I was occupying. I would pick up armfuls of papers and clothes and stuff them in the boxes lying around till they were full, then stack those boxes on top of other boxes and make sure they were stacked against the wall. I would take clothes lying around and dust the furniture then arrange the ornaments on the tables and shelves till they looked nice. I would clear the couches and chairs (ignoring the roaches that gave me the willies) and make it more presentable for someone to sit. Other times I went as far as taking the vacuum cleaner and vacuuming the now cleared space of floor and the furniture so I could sit and not feel uncomfortable. Other times when I came to the house (as the years went by), Jacob's brothers did the cleaning and clearing themselves if they knew I was coming, so they would not stand there with gaping jaws watching me clean their house and not know what to say or do.

Things at their house were a little more intense because Jacob's mom and dad would get involved. Because of my upbringing, I was not so volatile in my arguments with them there, but rather submissive and diluted. We would skim through passages of Bible verses, or Jacob's father would rehearse one story after another of Bible characters or individuals he had known within his life that had been touched by God. Jacob's mother would turn on various programs on TV and have me sit down and watch and learn, or she would play videos of various musical artists and encourage me to listen and to join into the worship.

Despite the hoarding in their house, I found a warmth and a homeliness there that I lacked in my own family and home, and it was like a starving man being given food again. I gorged myself on the love and the fellowship that came out of that family. And when I was dropped off at home, I longed for more. But even hours after being dropped off at home, my father would come to my bedroom door and direct for me to go sit on the couch and his and my nightly ritual would start again, and I would have to work harder to hold back tears of hate and resentment and hunger for the love I just had hours previously. How could God be so loving when he dangled the very thing I was starving for in front of my face only to snatch it away the moment I got it? I was being drowned in darkness and light at the same time, and the pressure of this confusion was overwhelming. Could God love someone He had cursed?

Besides performing together and the nightly phone calls and the weekend visits from Jacob or him and his brothers, we would also go on excursions with his youth group or Samantha's and Shirley's youth group. We went to so many Christian concerts and Bill Gothard seminars. I was learning a lot about the Bible, and the opportunities to sing and demonstrate my talent were pouring in, but I was not a Christian, and despite appearances, I had no desire to be one. If God would not love me, and would only toy with my heart, then what was the point? I would sing about the love of Jesus like I knew it, but I was not going to be another of his puppets. The only desire I had was to know whether God really was a loving God, and if so, then why all the "this"? And if he was not a loving God, then what could I do to protect myself from all of the vices he kept throwing at me? I sang the songs about his love as well as any secular song about love because I wanted to make it and become a star. Going to the various concerts and watching the speakers and how they carried and presented themselves gave me so much inspiration and guidance for my own future. Being able to escape from my home life in a more tactile way was going to concerts or watching them on TV or listening to the radio. This made my ambitions stronger and my imagination deeper. My father would spank me with the grandfather belt just as hard as he wanted, and I endured it because I knew I was going to a concert or running away to Jacob's house for the evening or losing myself soon in a phone conversation with my best friend. Dad and God could torture me; I would not care. They could not hurt me anymore. I found my escape. "I can forget all this soon; I just have to endure," I would tell myself. And sure enough, hours later or a day or so later, I would be lost in an engulfing concert or swallowed up by another Christian seminar.

During the week at school, I felt like I was sitting back and watching me walk down the hall, go to class, endure the taunts and meanness of my classmates, and survive the bus ride home, and then my life would begin again the moment I picked up the phone and began to speak to Jacob. We even did our homework together and competed on that too.

When we both came of age, we got our first jobs at the same time! I went to work for McDonald's because a group of my classmates (Rambert was among them) were going down to the local McDonald's on Dale Boulevard to apply! Out of twelve of us, about six were hired, me included, but only four of us continued there for a while. Jacob went down to the marine yard in my area and applied there. He loved the water and ships and always wanted to go out to sea and visit faraway places and meet foreign people. Working a job meant meeting new people, more people, new experiences, and introducing a third world. An unknown world. But just like going up to New York over the summer, it was a lot of fun and no one cared about my looks—only that I showed up on time and did a good job. So I went out of my way to do the best job over everyone else.

Once my supervisor asked me to take a shovel and clean up the manure that a rider's horse left in the parking lot. She meant it as a joke, but I took the shovel and shoveled it all up and into the dumpster. I did not bat an eye. I just did it because I was told to do it and I made sure I got every smelly crumb up. When I was done, and I walked back in, I saw my coworkers had been watching me out the window along with the managers. They had nothing to say except for me to go take a break in the break room.

Jacob was working just as hard on his job cleaning boats, sometimes staying after hours till he was done. At times he would crash at my house and spend the night, sleeping in the basement. When those nights happened (which were few), Dad did not call me out to the living room, and I got sleep for that night. But those nights were few.

The day came when life would take a sudden unexpected turn. All of us have points in our lives that shape and determine our destiny. This was one of those times, like when my grandfather died. I was supposed to go on a televised music competition my music teacher had signed me up for. She and I were flying out to the city in the morning. It would be my first airplane flight. I was scared about flying on the plane, but I was over the world about being on national TV and competing against other kids vocally. I was confident enough to know I had it in the bag, but I worried about my plane crashing, like it did for Patsy Cline and for Buddy Holly. But that flight never happened.

My mother received a phone call that evening informing us that Grandpa died. In the last two years of his life he had become pretty lame and was relegated to a wheelchair, unable to speak and half the towering massive size he once was. My last visit with him was caring for this shriveled-up, angry old man who cussed, threw up, and had an accident on himself, but pleaded with puppy dog eyes for you not to leave him alone. I loved this man once when he was healthy and strong and stood six feet, four inches tall with massive broad shoulders, a booming voice, and a presence that frightened Bogart. But I did not like this "thing" sitting in the wheelchair cussing at my grandmother and smelling awful at the breakfast table. Now my hero was gone.

On the day he died, he got out of his wheelchair thinking he had a bad case of indigestion and was trying to ease his chest pain. He struggled to climb the twenty-plus steps of his brownstone to his bedroom against the rebukes of my grandmother. He reached the top step, sat down, and turned to Grandma and said, "This is as far as I can go," then slumped down onto the floor and died right there.

Grandma got Mrs. Paris, who lived next door and was a nurse, and she resuscitated him, but he never woke up. He laid in the hospital for a week brain dead, until Grandma pulled the plug. Now, in the middle of the night, we rushed to pack our suitcases and headed up the New Jersey Turnpike for New York City. It was the funeral for a king, and I soon forgot the competition I was supposed to be in. Instead, I sang "In the Garden" before hundreds of mourning relatives, business owners, and other "dignitaries" of my grandfather's acquaintances. I sang as if it were the music competition, and I left many in tears and surprised. I gave no thought that I was at a funeral, my grandfather's funeral. All that was important to me was that I was singing and demonstrating my talent, and that maybe this opportunity would lead to me singing before thousands, as a star.

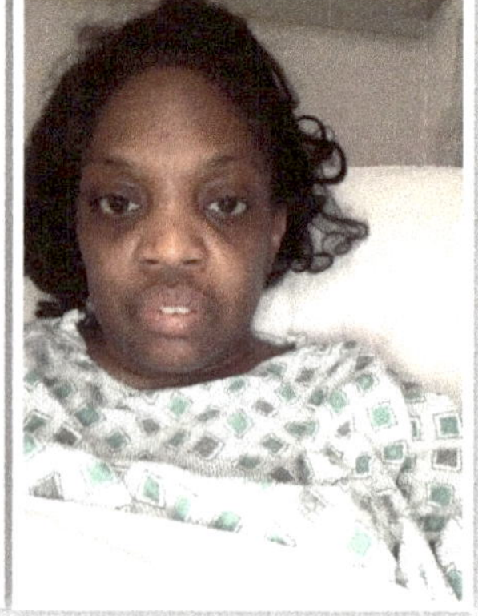

CHAPTER FOUR

The Hate In People

Dad's and Nathan's outbursts were becoming more heated and more frequent. Nathan grew a backbone as he got older, but his gentle soul was still no match for my father's fire. When my brothers and I became teenagers, Dad did not hold back from fighting with my brothers and forcing us all to be an audience. He would punch and slap them without mercy till they laid on the floor begging him to stop. No matter how much I cried and screamed for him to stop and get off my brothers, he would hit them harder and tell me to look at them and not turn away. When he would come and hit me till I was down on the ground, I would hide my face in my arms and roll up into a ball to protect myself. He would try to unravel me, and my brothers would yell for him to stop so he would go after them. It was always a mess. A godless mess.

But Nathan still fell apart at the first insult. Dad never had to hit him; his words hurt Nathan deep. Nathan could not take it anymore, and at one point he rode his rusty orange bike all the way down Route 11 to a counselor's office, forced himself into the man's office, and begged for help, crying pitifully. Dad was fit to be tied when that happened but went to the counseling meetings for a time. When we all sat in the waiting room, he would threaten all of us that if we said one thing in any way negative, we would truly get it when we got home, so we were silent for the most part. Dad did all the speaking. We went about three or four times before Dad squashed it.

On the day Dad put an end to the counseling, Nathan ran out of the house, got in his car, and drove to Manassas, which was a distance away from us. He watched some children playing in their yard, and having a child's mentality himself (he was 17 but mentally he was more like 8 at the time) he went into their backyard to play with them on their swing set when they invited him to come. Their mother saw the strange black man in her yard playing with her innocent little boys and called the police. She accused Nathan of fondling and molesting her three boys. Nathan was arrested and sent to detention center. We got the call about Nathan and the notice to appear in court. If that was not bad enough, we showed up on the front pages of the Potomac News: my brother's name and our address. Some reporter mistakenly thought my brother was eighteen. He was seventeen. Overnight we were infamous. It was not the fame I or my family wanted.

CHAPTER FIVE

A Letter to My Daughter

Dear Rachel,

Rachel, I want you to know, if you do not know already, first that I love you; I want you to know that what you did 15 years ago was heroic. You did the best thing you could ever do, you saved us all, you did the right thing, you went to the authorities and you cried out for help, and you saved your family. And I never got to tell you thank you. I am sorry you went through that. I am sorry that you got hurt. The details of everything are not important. What is important is that you know that I am sorry that it happened and that you got hurt. For the last 15 years, I have been so sorry that it happened to you. I want to ask for your forgiveness for not being there to protect you. I was not there to protect you. I am so sorry. I want to help you heal and to get better.

You thought I walked out on you, but I did not abandon you; I did not. My father did not want me to stay in the house. He kicked me out. Being in a shelter was no place for children. I did not want any of you there, a homeless shelter. In addition, that is why I did not take you with me. I did not want you to be in a homeless shelter. However, I have never forgotten that day when I had to leave you. I wanted you to be with me. I had to tell you no, and I knew you did not understand why I had to leave. In addition, I could not tell you. I did not want you to look badly at your grandfather, and I was not going to take you to stay at a homeless shelter with me. Now, I am glad I made that decision. You had been through a lot, and I knew you were safe at your grandfather's house. I was not going to take you children. It was better for me to live homeless on the street, and not for you children to be there. I would have never forgiven myself as a mother.

You had been through a lot—when we were able to be a family again, I knew you did not understand, and I knew you were angry and did not want to forgive me. You thought I walked out and abandoned you. From your eyes, your point of view, it looked like I abandoned you, and I am sorry. There is no way to fix that or make it better. By 2006, I just wanted our family back together again, but by then, I had lost you. I just want you to know I have not forgotten you. I never can. You are my daughter. I have never forgotten you. I cannot. I want you to be in my life. I think it is important for you to know. I do not reject you. You were a kid, and as a kid, you did the right thing and I

am thankful to you for going to the authorities. I will always love you, Rachel, and I hope one day you will choose to come home and be part of our lives again.
Merry Christmas Rachel.
Unsent letter November 23, 2017

I had never seen so many angry people in my completely short life. I was young when my brother went to court for a crime he did not commit. Nathan looked thin and helpless, his eyes lost and empty sitting beside his lawyer, an overweight, not well-dressed, and greasy-haired individual with an unkempt briefcase and thick black-rimmed glasses. I do not remember anything said within that courtroom. I remember the adults looked bigger and more menacing than anything I saw on TV. I did not like these adults. There were women in tight suits, stockings, and heels, yelling and pushing their way. There were men in very sharp suits and leather shoes arguing and growling at anyone and anything. There were all kinds of smells and so much sadness on the face of so many. I saw a few church friends from our church at Ecclesiastical and Reverend Jones, but no one was smiling like at church. I was very frightened by the whole thing, especially the distant look on my mother's face, like someone told her Nathan was dying and all was hopeless. I did not know what to make of any of this. Where was this loving God? Is my brother Nathan cursed too, or was this my fault?

Things changed at home. Mom and Dad were arguing very loudly, or they were eerily quiet for hours. Mom would sit in her room in the dark. Dad would stare at the TV and not really listen to anything. Other times we would come home from school and find Dad passed out on the hallway floor or the living room floor. He would be sloppily drunk. Cliff and I or Brian and I would help Dad up and back to his room on his bed. It became a regular thing to come home and find Dad passed out. I was thankful when Mrs. Blue offered to allow me to stay at her house after school because she thought I would like to hang out with her girls. She was right.

Life at school got worse too. Our family situation made the front page of the Petromax News. The kids at school were as mean and menacing as the adults in the courtroom. My whole world filled up with mean and angry people. On my locker, I would receive cruel notes telling me I was ugly or a monster or how I needed to die. I would have kids threaten to kill me and how they would do it. I would receive notes telling me to kill myself and how I should do it. I would get several notes from kids simply saying they hated me. In class, I had kids throw pennies and paper balls at me. They loved rolling my name off their tongues in all the derogatory ways that they could think of. In the bathrooms or locker rooms, I would be hit, punched, slapped, or spit upon. Many times on the steps I got pushed down or hit on the back of my head, or I had hate notes shoved into my hand. The bus was worse because I could not get away. Some of the kids would turn around in their seat and insist I say what they wanted me to say. I would refuse and get slapped for it. They would keep slapping me until I cried. Corey Jones, Reverend Jones older son, would sit with me deliberately so the kids would back off and leave me alone. My days and nights became a blur of crying tears constantly.

There were a few places I found sanctuary, including the choir room where we sang. I was one of the best singers the school had, so the music took me away from my problems. No one knew me as Fea Khan, sister of Nathan and Cliff Khan. In the choir room, I was whomever the music made me into.

Another sanctuary was the art room. I had my hecklers that would dog me at times, but once I began working on a project, I was overtaken by the art and lost within the work.

Another sanctuary was the drama club. Part of that club was the debate team and the "United Nations" (UN), and I belonged to both of them. When I got into the zone of a debate, it was all that existed before me—the argument. I was thorough in my research and discussing the topic at hand; it was what I lived for. With extemporaneous speaking and acting out a character, I would lose myself within the story and the emotion I wanted to display. It was like singing; the song pulls the emotions out of your audience, and the melody takes you on a ride, whether you wish to go or not. I liked being lost in this way. It was a safe drug, a safe getaway. I threw myself into debating and forensic and won trophy after trophy. I sang loud and strong, throwing my voice literally to the back of the room, then pulling it back and wrapping it around myself as if to remind my listener that it was mine and no one else's. The stage was the only place I could smile; I could control my world. There was no fear on that stage, only the power to change all the ugliness into beauty once again. The stage became my sanctuary. I was God and I would show God what love was in my songs.

Another sanctuary was my job. Once I turned 15, there was a group of us that decided to go and get a job at the same time. Over lunch we would discuss where would be a good place to start. We had mutual English and social studies teachers who happened to be husband and wife, and it allowed us kids to bounce employment ideas off them. We all concluded that McDonald's would be a good starting place. Back then, your first job was commonly babysitting, a newspaper route, and working at a fast-food restaurant. Most of us around 12 had worked as babysitters or as newspaper boys/girls. Now we were ready to move to the next level, working a real job at a fast-food restaurant. Six of us marched down to McDonald's on Dale Boulevard, and four of us were hired on the spot. The day I began working at McDonald's, eight of my classmates and friends were there too. Working at McDonald's was like going to a civic center and playing volleyball with your best friends into the night. It was sheer joy and fun. We worked the register, stocked, mopped floors, and made burgers; we worked the jobs, but it was just a lot of fun. And the people we ran into, the things people said and did, or the things children did in the lobby, it was overwhelming life, and it took me away from my painful shyness, the alcoholic problems at home, and the court issues we were being made to live through.

Being at my job gave me a taste of what life could be like outside of the high school walls where the bullies ruled, and I was nothing but a piece of dirt under their feet. I reveled in being a cashier and then later a hostess at McDonald's. I worked hard to win employee of the month and other smaller awards McDonalds would give during that time. McDonald's helped build my personal self-esteem despite the other terrible things going on in my life. While I worked there on Fridays and Saturdays, I worked as an afterschool daycare attendant at Dale City Christian Church Monday through Thursday for four hours. I was not a Christian at the time, but Reverend Jones had done so much for our family by way of befriending my dad. Dad never slammed the door on Reverend Jones, and many times he had dinner with us. When I began working, I first began working at a day care run by a member of Ecclesiastical Lutheran Church. I worked there for a while. But for some reason, I switched over to Dale City Christian Church when it first opened its day care. Being an after-school assistant to the teacher made me feel very important, responsible, and mature. I was considering becoming a teacher after graduation to please my mom (but I was still working out running away to California), so this worked in my plans.

These sanctuaries brought me peace during all the chaos going on in my life at the time. Looking back, music and drama on the stage, my art and writing, and working a job outside of home were my drugs of choice. I hit these drugs hard, I took these drugs religiously, and I could not live without any of these. I awoke and I went to sleep on these drugs, and without just one of these, I would go down a road of self-destruction.

CHAPTER SIX

From Moon to Khan

As a kid of an alcoholic father, my brothers and I were the poster children of child abuse. At some point, my father had a religious epiphany and became an alcoholic Muslim/ Freemason. Dad worked at the Lotan Correctional Center as Captain; previously, he was a police officer for Prince William County. But the racism he confronted, the low pay, and the demeaning work he was given as an officer led him to pursue becoming a correctional officer. There, my father had ample opportunity to climb the ladder of promotion, becoming the best in every position he held until he became captain. There at Lorton, my father ruled. Like my grandfather before him, Dad had men that surrounded him, were loyal to him, and came to him for favors; others were forever ruined by one word out of my father's twisted heart. Dad found his kingdom, and our home was truly his castle. When my father left work, to come home, he forgot he was at home and not in the prison. Though Dad took his officer hat off and laid his baton down, he still walked the halls of our home as Captain Pete Khan. There was no father.

My mother was the opposite. She was a hugger extraordinaire and lover of everyone; however, she was helpless in the face of my father's tantrums and threats towards her. Mom worked for the FBI and was a churchgoer on Sundays. Sunday mornings were all about communion, confirmation, suits, red Bibles, and puffy dresses; all before noon. Then life went back to normal: lock-and-key kids during the weekdays and terrorized frightened abused children by night. My mother was exactly what you met when she walked into a room. She was a bright light. Her voice was soft and kind. She was winsome and attractive; a friend to the friendless. Mom thought of others before herself and was moved to action when she met someone who was in need. When we were young, faith was not the center of my mother's life, but you would have thought it was. She was a living Bible without knowing Jesus personally. Mom gave all of herself to her children and those she loved around her. But because of her empty spiritual life, enduring Dad and his piercing personal attacks were heartbreaking for her. There were many days and afternoons we would find Mom sitting in the dark of her room, crying. She did not understand why Dad was so hateful when she worked so hard to be so loving. It was always overwhelming hearing my mother weeping on her bed.

My father and I had a secret at night. My father would come home and visit me in my room at night. I could feel his shadow at my room door. I knew what my father wanted, and I braced myself in hopes that he would be nice to my brothers and I if I was a good girl. My father started molesting me at age five and continued into my teenage years. My father began molesting me when he and my mother stopped sleeping together. Mom took on the back room and Dad kept the master bedroom. They did not kiss anymore, nor hug or hold hands. When I was a toddler, Dad would chase Mom around the house, and Mom would laugh when Dad caught her and kissed her. We would hear them behind the door making love in the afternoon. But after one very heated argument ending in my mother weeping pitifully and Grandpa threatening my father's life if ever he did whatever it was that he did, Mom and Dad never got close to each other ever again. Mom moved out of their room, and Dad came and visited me in my room that first week. He continued to visit me, molesting me at the beginning and talking continuously about all his ghosts until I turned fourteen. After I went into puberty, he would come to my room and tell me to go sit on the couch in the living room. There he would talk continuously about the things that made him mad and frustrated. By the time he had drunk his fourth moose cup of Jack Daniels, he would slur his words or say things that made no sense. I would sit there frozen, afraid to move or get up until he fell asleep. We continued this sick daughter/father ritual until I married Jacob and moved away at nineteen.

As I mentioned earlier, in my teen years I tried out for Duke Ellington School of Performing Arts and I was accepted on my vocals and my art. For six weeks I bathed in the reality that being a performer could be my future. It was the best six weeks of my life. Then my father found out about the secret shared between my mother and me. He pulled me out and put me into the local school where racial tension and bullying were kings. My brothers and I were daily beaten up in various fights, most during lunch time. Some of them made the Petromax newspaper, and others were even on the evening news. In one incident, a black boy stuck a fork into the neck of a white boy. Another time, a group of blacks and whites were fighting it out in the middle of the lunchroom, and a group of us ran out to avoid being harmed. I was surrounded by a group of white girls on the stairs. I braced myself expecting the blows to come to my head when I heard some yelling and screaming. I opened my eyes to see a group of black girls beating up the white girls that had chased me. When they had chased them away, I started to excitedly thank them for their help, but they dismissed my words away. They were angry with me. I was a disgrace to the culture, a mistake, they said. They proceeded to beat me up themselves. When I came home with a black eye and bruises on my body, my father was only concerned about the broken pair of glasses I held in my hand. I was lined up against his bedroom wall and whipped till blood streamed down my legs. I became depressed and embittered. I hated my parents, but mostly, I hated God.

After the incident mentioned earlier where Nathan was arrested and falsely charged, we were mercilessly attacked by the public and in school. Our life up to this point was nothing compared to the hell we began to live. My father became a fall-out drunk, and my mother would sit alone in the dark of her room and cry non-stop. We no longer had any parents. We began to raise ourselves.

Things had become so frightening at home and at school that we did nothing to protect or look after each other. Brian began to work at a bar at the age of fourteen. He lied about his age, but when his age was discovered, they let him continue working there because his work ethic was so impressive. Cliff began working two jobs, one on base and another at Burger King. If he were not working, he would hang out with his friends then sneak back home, undetected by Mom and Dad. They did not care anymore. I worked three jobs: McDonalds, the church daycare, and a newspaper route (I later had to let that go because of what happened to my brother, and I started selling Avon). When I was not working, I just stayed within the halls of the community church and listened to the pastor going over his sermon for the week.

As a result of what was going on with my brother, a boy from my school and a swing manager raped me one night after work. My brother Cliff was supposed to pick me up from work after he got off. Instead he went home and fell asleep. He never received my calls. I was hesitant to ride with my manager. I knew he was giving Danny and others a ride home too. Danny had tried to attack me previously twice in the stock room. He waited till I had to go back into the stock room for cups or other things. He would come up behind me and push me against the wall. He would force a kiss on me while his hands struggled to undress me and feel me. I had to fight to get him off. He only pulled away when someone else walked into the room. I quickly ran away back to the front and fought to calm my shaking down while taking another person's order. The second time I was saved by a friend who came to my rescue. He once again had pushed me up against the wall, but I struggled fiercely. He got me down on the ground and was working very hard to undo my pants and his own. I could not get him off from on top of me, and he forced his kiss on my mouth and would not let up. Then I felt another hand around Danny's throat and his body being lifted off of me. It was our mutual friend, Gil. Once He pulled Danny off me, I got up, fixed my pants, and ran out.

Nothing was ever said between the three of us about what happened. I tried to tell my manager, Smithy, about it. I was afraid to work at the same time with Danny. He laughed and assumed it was just a lover's quarrel. So, I told my best friend, Jacob. He was furious. Jacob and his brothers came to McDonald's and confronted him. They scared him into leaving me alone. But a rumor was going around school where the boys were betting each other to see who could be first to force sex on "Fea" in retaliation for what they assumed my brother did.

I had had others attempt to put me in questionable positions because I was naïve, but none were successful. Danny was the only one that had taken it too far, and he got my manager, Smithy, to help him. After my manager dropped all the others off, Danny and I were alone in the back seat of Mr. Smithy's car. He turned the music up, and Danny attacked me as we drove down Dale Boulevard. Danny was on top and inside me when our manager pulled the car to the side and told Danny to get out. "But you promised," he complained like a child having dessert withheld from him. Mr. Smithy forced him to walk home then told me to redress and get up front. I cleaned the tears from my face and thanked him abundantly for stopping the rape. I was still shaking as I saw him drive past my house and into the woods on Doppler Road.

"Well you said you are thankful; why don't you show me?" he said.

I started crying again. He told me to get quiet or my father would come out and be angry with me. I do not know why that fear was more overwhelming than what this 30-year-old first lieutenant in the Army did to me, but the threat of my dad coming out and yelling at me made me freeze. When he was done, he told me to get out and made me walk home in the dark. He drove away in his shiny white 1978 Cadillac. I walked silently alone in the dark under the stars and a bright oval moon, strongly believing that there could not be a God. God was supposed to be loving. How was this loving? God was supposed to protect His children. He did not protect me. God was supposed to be a father. God was not a father to me, as my own father was not a father to me. I was alone in this world, and no one cared for me. I came home and fell silent. For months I sat at home, excessively washing, refusing to eat, and searching for ways to kill myself.

Our home became unbearable. We began to go to family counseling once more. My mother was able to find support for herself through the local church family, but I stayed silent. The psychologist suggested I go to a youth group and back to school. I refused to go to school. I would not leave my room nor go to eat. I had lost a lot of weight, and my hair was beginning to fall out. My mother had no power to get me to go back to school. I refused to tell either one of them what had happened to me, but the psychologist guessed it had to be something horrible, such as rape. My mother was devastated by the hurt and pain she saw in me and in my brother, Nathan, when we went to visit him. The first few months, they mistakenly put him with the grown men. Something terrible happened there, and, like me, he never spoke of it, but the light in his eyes had gone out. He was dead, like me. Nathan barely talked when we went to visit him. I barely talked at all.

My father forced me on the bus after dressing me against my will. He could not take my awkward silence and my mother's constant crying. He avoided visiting Nathan, but he could not avoid the lack of my presence and the low quiet mourning of my mother day and night. He pulled me off my bed, dragged me down the hallway with my mother screaming "Evan! Stop!" He pulled my clothes off me, ripping the neck of my nightgown accidentally. He picked my boney body up and dropped it into the porcelain bathtub, then he turned the shower water on. It was shocking. I started screaming, too. He picked up the soap, but Mom took his arm and screamed she would do it. She washed me all over against my will, then dried me off. I was crying and saying "No, leave me alone!", but I was ignored. Dad came back in with school clothes and Mom gave them to me to put on, which I did. All the while, Dad

went outside in his police officer uniform, and when the bus came, he stopped it from turning the corner by holding up his hand. He got on the bus and told the driver to wait. She obeyed. Dad came back in and grabbed my arm. He dragged me down the stairs and out into the light of day. Then he dragged me onto the bus, tears pouring down my face and shocked looks from all my schoolmates.

"Take her to school, you hear me?" he said.

"Yes, sir," the driver said.

The entire bus was silent for the whole ride to school. Many of my schoolmates, even the ones who had bullied me, gave me their apologies as they got off the bus once we got to school. I would not get off the bus on my own. I was deeply afraid and shaking as if I were cold. They took me directly to the counselor's room and worked for hours to help me calm down. From that day until close to graduation, the principal and student counselor allowed me to finish the rest of my class for school in the principal's office. It was my first bout with agoraphobia.

I continued to stay silent at school, and now at home. I was forced to go to the youth group at Dale City Baptist Church as instructed by the psychologist. The first night, I would not let go of the door once I stepped inside the room. Before I came in, they were all laughing and talking about something. A gregarious, charismatic, effeminate man named Mr. Gabriel Wonder walked over to me and took my hand; he invited me to sit with him and to not be afraid. I was afraid. He took my hand and I pulled away, refusing to look at him or anyone else.

"No one is going to hurt you, darling," Gabriel said. "We are all friends here. Right guys?"

There was a low mumble of agreement.

"Yeah, thanks guys, that is really believable."

Everyone laughed, even me.

"There it is. There is that smile. I promise you, if any of these monsters try to hurt you, I will hang them upside down by their toenails." That made me laugh too. I let him take my hand, and I sat next to him through the whole class. Gabriel became my guardian angel; he became my super man and the one I looked up to from that point on.

One afternoon, July 1, 1986, I was attempting suicide once more when I heard Billy Graham on the TV. I had attempted in many ways but was never successful. I would wake up disappointed. The Reverend Billy Graham was preaching about the Lordship of Christ and our need for a Savior. ***He talked about how we do a lousy job at determining our lives. We make so many mistakes, from the beginning of time. Instead of obeying the Creator, we wanted to be like God, so we chose disobedience, and sin came into the world. He said sin is not the answer to our problems. God is the creator of all the world; He holds the blueprints. He has a plan for each of our lives, and His desire is for each of us to affect one another with Love, the love of God. When He is the captain of our ship, He knows which way our rutter needs to turn. He will take us down which way we need to go, and no matter the trial we go through, He will never leave us alone. He will always comfort us and heal us if we reach out to Him.***

God loves us, and no matter what we do or whatever comes into our lives, He will be there with us and make a way of escape for us. God knew we would fail at being our own saviors. No matter how hard we try or how close we think we can get, we are lousy at being the Lord and Savior over our lives. Sin is more powerful than any of us, and Satan has the corner on

wielding that tool against us. We are no match for him in the spiritual world on our own. God, out of His overwhelming and irresistible love for us, knew this and made a way for us to escape the fate we chose for ourselves when we decided as humans to sin against God. God gave us Jesus.

Jesus put His glory and sovereignty aside and came into this world, born a helpless infant so he could empathize with our hurts, pain, and lives. Jesus was born to die. For our sin to be satisfied, the price for it had to be paid. That price was death. Jesus paid the price for death with His own life. He lived sinlessly, completing what Adam was unable to do, then He willingly laid down His life for us. He took on all our sins from the past, the present, and the future so we could be forgiven of all our sins. All sin was laid on Jesus on the Cross for me while I was still an enemy of God. God did this not because there was something special in me or because He knew I would choose to turn to Him. God did this completely out of His overwhelming love for me. He wants me to have joy, to be safe and protected, and he wanted me to have all the best there was in life to have. If I were willing to turn to Him with my sins, repent, and humbly acknowledge that I needed a savior and that I could do nothing without the Lord, if I trusted and believed in the sacrificial cross work of Christ for me, then God would save me. He would renew me in my heart and in my mind. He would teach me wisdom, love, kindness, patience, gentleness, longsuffering, and self-control towards myself and others. He would give me the free gift of forgiveness when I sin, grace even when I don't deserve it, and mercy so that I could learn to do the same towards others, and he would give me the precious gift of prayer so He might speak with me and show me all of His heart as I chose to be obedient to His will and honor His word in my life through my actions, my thoughts, and my behavior.

I needed a way of escape out of my pain and hurt and the overwhelming shame and guilt I felt from my rapes. What stood out for me were the words, "When your mother and father forsake you, the Lord, He will take you up." It opened the floodgates for me and softened my heart because I felt abandoned by my mother and father. They were not there to protect me. They were caught up in the situation with my brother Nathan. I had no parents, and it had become a sad and lonely existence for me and my brothers. I did not want to live anymore. In my heart, I was always crying. No one wanted me, and now, after this, no one would want me or accept me for who I was now: broken and cursed. The Reverend Billy Graham talked about a God who knew me and loved me for who I was. He accepted me in all my brokenness and wanted to heal me. He not only created me; He was my father. He said our Heavenly Father gives us good gifts. That His love was everlasting and irresistible. I wanted to know this God who loved me despite my trying to kill myself. He loved me despite my being raped and being no good to anyone else.

I felt I could say nothing to my parents about what happened, my salvation. We were still in the middle of

Nathan's court case. I cried out to God and asked Him to forgive me for the wrong things I had done. At the time, I felt the rape was my fault. I felt so much guilt and shame. I was haunted by overwhelming fear and pain. I could not look in people's faces. What if it happened again? Could I ever get my virginity back? I wanted children and a husband, but I was damaged. Who would want me? I asked Him to please help me handle the wrongs that had been done to me and to take me up as He had promised. My hate and bitterness fell away that day as I became a new creation before all of heaven.

After high school I tried out for Julliard and was accepted on my talent. I made the trip up to New York by bus and stayed with my grandmother in her brownstone. Grandpa had been gone for five years by then. My grandmother was doing very well for herself and stayed active within her church as a missionary. We spent many evenings talking about how God is a good father to His children and His overwhelming love for us. My grandmother was elated that I was a new Christian, but she also warned me that my dad's response to me being a Christian may not be what I am expecting. She warned me I may face more rejection than I do now.

"Becoming a Christian is a wonderful thing," she said. "Life does not get easier; it gets harder, but you will never be alone. God is always with you and He will never stop loving you."

On my first day to Julliard, my grandmother was very proud of me. Mom called to let me know how proud of me she was. I was very excited. I felt like I brought a little bit of light into the life of my family. Maybe this will be my time, finally. Maybe I do have worth. Maybe I am not cursed after all. Maybe God had finally healed my brokenness, and maybe going to Julliard proved I could be whole. I could be valuable to my parents, especially my dad. When I had come up to New York to try out, no one came with me. No one was devoted to the idea of me going to Julliard any longer and becoming a famous musician. The trauma of my brother's arrest and incarceration swallowed up any hope or aspirations any of us had. Only my grandmother's constant reminder of what lay ahead in my future kept me pursuing this school of performing arts. When the letter of acceptance came in the mail, no one celebrated. I held it to myself and shared it with my grandmother. She called my mom and shared with her the good news. My mother hugged me and told me, good job. Dad only learned of it on the day I prepared to pack and go live with my grandmother. His answer to me was that I would be back.

I did part of the first day and left. There was no reason for me to leave. I stood in that long red hall and looked up those long red steps with all the students shuffling here and there, racing towards their classes, and I panicked. Being surrounded by that many people and having the huge expectation on my shoulders to do well, it was more than I could bear. I raced to the women's room and hid in a stall for hours. Sitting on the toilet, I cried, hugging myself. I wished I could call my grandmother and hear her voice, but I was too scared to leave. I did not go back ever again.

It was my first bout with agoraphobia. My grandmother prayed over me that evening and encouraged me to go back, but I would not. I was not ready. My parents and my grandmother were disappointed. They had invested so much into me. No one understood the change that had overcome me. I never said anything about what happened that night, not even to my grandmother. I turned deep inside myself. I embraced depression, and my thoughts were very dark. I cut off many of my friends and associates—not purposely; I just did not keep up contacts. Not only was I cursed and broken, but now I was a failure. I could not look my parents in the face. Neither one of them said anything about my aborting my Julliard career.

Determined to see me go to college, my parents sent me to Newberry College in South Carolina after I obtained a scholarship from the local Lutheran church for my academics. A month later, I sat in South Carolina, far away from everything and everyone that was familiar. I did well in the beginning in South Carolina. There were plenty of open places without crowds of people. The surrounding scenery was calming and beautiful, especially during the sunrise. I spent a lot of my time within the campus sanctuary. When I sang, my voice would echo loudly. I loved the sound I heard. It made me feel like I was surrounded by the angels. When I would go to the chapel and sing, I would spend hours there, and it would ease my nerves. It was comforting. I lived in the library and sanctuary on campus and stayed mostly to myself. I became very odd, set apart. My professors did not know what to do with me. Academically, I was bright and highly intelligent. But getting me to show up for classes was like pulling hair out. But they could not truly complain, because if you wanted to find me, I was in the library lost in books and studying, or singing my heart out in the sanctuary. Late in the evening, when classes were over and everyone had left to go to the dorms or to go have dinner, I would sneak down the empty halls, past the janitors, and leave my work for that day, either on the desk of my professors, or in their mailbox if it was attached to their door. When we had to take a quiz or a test, I showed up, sitting in the front of the class, by the professor's desk. Some of the surprised looks on their faces was priceless. Once I completed the quiz or test, I would quickly leave out of the classroom. Most said nothing. Only once did I have a professor pursue me out of the class and reach for my arm. I jumped away very quickly. "Vicky, I'm sorry, my class is not over. Stay and participate. You might find you like it." His smile was gentle and inviting for an older gentleman, but my mind was made up. I shook my head and kept on down the hall and out the door into the inviting sunlight.

One night I had a mental/emotional breakdown as agoraphobia began to take over once more. The community was at a basketball game. I was found outside in the middle of the night in my night gown while it was snowing, crying and crying out like a prophet. I screamed at everyone coming out of the game that they all were doomed to hell because of their unfaithful life to God. The population was returning from a big basketball game when they were confronted by me in my thin pink and blue nightgown. I wept and begged them to repent of the sin in their heart and to stop disobeying God. I was sincere in my begging of them, as if we were drowning men in a ship going down. The coach put a jacket over me, settled me down and carried me back to my dorm while a huge crowd watched. I clung to him as if he were my father and I was a little girl. I hid my face into his chest so I would not see all the observers staring. I was very sick in my heart and mind. For a week I lay in my dorm bed burning up with fever from the flu. The campus nurse doctored me back to physical health. The campus counselor was deeply concerned for my mental stability. She and the campus chaplain tried very hard to get me to talk about the weight on my heart that burdened me so heavily, but I stayed tight-lipped. The school determined it would be best to send me home. I failed again. Jacob was back home from college. He got a four-year ride to Texas A&M. He met me at the bus stop in South Carolina and I ran to him, my long-lost friend. We hugged for a very long time. On that long bus ride home, I held onto Jacob and erased any thoughts of where I was going, back home. The only things that existed for the both of us going home were Keith Green, Sandi Patti, and the scenery.

While I figured out what do with myself, Mom and I went to a Bill Gothard seminar together. Mom hoped it would help me snap out of it. Bill Gothard was well known in evangelical circles for being a great teacher in Christian living and ethics. Because his lessons were pragmatic and analytical, they rang true with my mother and struck a chord in her heart. For the first time in her life, she recognized that the God of the Bible her mother had spoken to her about so arduously was the God she did not know. She wanted to know Him more and know Him personally. I watched tears quietly come down my mother's face many times throughout the seminar. By the third day of the seminar in DC, during a break time, Mom confessed she did not know Jesus like Mr. Gothard had talked about him. She went to church because that is what you do. It is safe. But a close relationship with God? God as her father? She never thought it was possible, but she wanted it. We prayed together on that grassy knoll, and my mother became a born-again Christian.

I enrolled at Northern Virginia Community College (NOVA) and worked two jobs to stay away from my violent and lascivious father. My mother was a new Christian at that time, but her relationship with me was not enough to make my home safe. When mom became a Christian, I took the opportunity to announce to my dad that I was a Christian, too. He hated me for it and blamed me for putting such foolishness in my mother's mind. I must want my mother to be crazy like me too, he said. He insisted that I let go of this born-again garbage that the preachers at the prison preach, or he would not be my father anymore. I could not let God go. I did not want to be a Muslim or an Eastern Star. We had many very heated nights over religion, as my father attempted to shred any amount of faith and hope I had in my heart for Jesus and His promises towards me. To be able to stand up against my dad, I would write my questions down and go to the library and research the answers in scripture.

My father's lascivious side was another thing. He wanted to continue our ritual I had escaped from when I left to go live with Grandma. I felt like I could not tell him no, and I feared getting beat by my father again. So, I laid silent until he was done, then I dutifully got up, joined him in the living room and continued to listen to his war stories, hate, and regret. The room would fill with his cigarette smoke, and I felt suffocated. I longed for the sunrises, the silence, the echoing halls of the chapel, the countless shelves of books, and the smell of paper within them. I missed the hours of walking alone by the lake and the laughter of my friends in the prayer group I attended. I wanted to go back to my life, but when it was offered to me after Christmas, I would not get on the bus and go back. I had to get away from my dad; I had to get away from my failures and shame. But how?

CHAPTER SEVEN

Marriage?

I hastily chose to marry my friend, Jacob, when he courted me and then asked. It was unnatural. I was not attracted to him in that way. I was not attracted to anyone. He was my best friend, my brother. How could he be my husband? How could I be a wife? I only said yes to marrying him to get away from my father, who would not leave me alone. Jacob was the only one I opened up to about the rapes when I came back home. I told him I did not think I could be a good wife in that regard because of what happened. I had no desire for sex. Jacob thought he could help me. I thought, here is my best friend. Who better to live my life with than my best friend? Besides, after the agoraphobic attacks and the mental breakdown, I could only see myself becoming a teacher. Jacob asked for my hand three times. The fourth time, I told him to ask my parents. I figured either he would not ask, and would get discouraged, or they would say no. He took me up on my challenge and asked my dad. Dad said yes and so did Mom. We married December 9, 1989. I hoped this wedding would make up for all my failures and would finally make me a blessing to my dad instead of a curse to my family. Maybe my father would talk to me again.

Reverend Jones refused to do the ceremony on the day of my wedding, which is why I was in that Sunday school room waiting. When Jacob and I arrived, he called us in. He yelled at us for putting a wedding together where both parents were not in agreement. He was especially upset with me that I did not tell him Jacob's dad did not approve of the match. I had no idea his father felt that way, and I made a call to the reverend to let him know so much. I burst into uncontrollable tears. The secretary heard my outburst and escorted me out of the reverend's office and into the Sunday school room I was waiting in. I waited for three hours not knowing whether my wedding would happen or not. The reverend's reaction seemed to prove that I was a curse to everyone, and that no matter what I did, there was no way I could get away from my fate. Maybe Jacob and I should not get married. Maybe I should just run away and try to make it on my own. Looking back, if I had thought through my tears, I would have seen that God made a way of escape for me. A wedding was not the way He would use to free me from living at home with my predatorial father, and saying no to the wedding could have been my first step toward true freedom. But I could not see it at the time, and the wedding was back on when a visiting pastor came and offered to do the ceremony for us. Soon my father was escorting me down the aisle looking very proud and happy.

Jacob was in the Navy and stationed at Bethesda Naval Hospital, working towards becoming a pharmacist. Our life in Gaithersburg started out simple. We were kids playing house for real, with no furniture. At night after work, we would play hide-and-go-seek, chess, and various board games we got at the local Goodwill. Other times we would read the Bible out loud and pretend to be the different characters. When it was time to shower, and then time to go to bed, Jacob would try to be intimate with me. But I would refuse him. I could not bring myself to have sex with my husband. Jacob was very frustrated. He had looked forward for a long time to become one with me. After three months we went to the library and checked out a book that showed us different ways for making love. When I saw how it was done, the memories of what had happened to me came flooding back. I screamed and closed the book.

"Jacob I cannot do that," I said. "Please understand. I did not realize this is what was expected of me as your wife."

"How can you say that you did not know?" Jacob replied. "This is how a husband and wife show each other how much they love one another. So let me show you, and maybe you will not be so afraid."

"No, I cannot do that," I said. "It will hurt. And I do not want to hurt like that. It is awful. And I do not want us to ever have to do this. Please promise me you will not make me."

"But what about me?" said Jacob. "Don't I matter? I want to know what it is like—but with you, not anybody else. It is not fair to make me live like this."

"But Jacob, I thought we were friends."

"We are friends. But this friend also wants to be treated like a husband and have sex with his wife."

The evening did not go well for us. We disagreed way into the night being the debaters that we were. Neither one of us in our immaturity considered how our actions might hurt the other in the long run. Jacob was patient for another month, but after four months he decided to force me to have sex with him whether I wanted to or not.

It was not a romantic evening. I spent the rest of the night crying in a corner of the bathroom. But for Jacob the joy of having sex for the first time was addictive. From that evening forward Jacob demanded sex each night, whether I wanted to or not. And his brother Immanuel, who had come to live with us since his job was in the area where we lived, supplied Jacob with the necessary scripture verses he needed to justify his forcing the situation against my will. Five months later, when I contemplated no longer being married, we discovered I was pregnant. I cried and weeped as if someone were dying. I told my parents that I was pregnant, and they were over the moon. They had always dreamed of having a "gram baby." And I would be the first of their children to make their dream possible. My father spoke to me, but only about his grandbaby and when it would soon be due. How could I tell them about what I had lived through for the last eight months? I could not. Jacob was not punching me or slapping me. He was just insisting on what I was required to do as a wife. Right. I made a covenant between him and God vowing to be a faithful wife to him before God. If I left him now, I would break my parents' hearts and my father would stop talking to me again. I just could not do it. Dad had not talked to me in close to five years. I was his biggest failure and disappointment. I would be an even bigger disappointment and failure to my father, my mother, my grandmother, and God. No, I could not do it. So, I stayed and endured. There were many nights where I faked being OK. Jacob would enjoy what he was doing and then fall asleep on top of me until he was ready to begin again. I would lay there and look up into the light that was on the ceiling and place myself there. There I would sit and watch every little detail that was happening to me below. I would watch and say nothing. But I would cry for the me that was trapped under the sleeping Jacob.

We moved eight times within a short period because of Jacob's financial irresponsibility. I never expected the instability. I slowly stopped calling and visiting my parents because I was ashamed. We did not stay in one place for more than a year. At home we were like kids. We had no furniture most of the time for the first three years. Once home, after work, we would play hide-and-go-seek, chess, and various card and board games. We went running in the park, took long walks, and ate out. We listened to *Unshackled!* and acted out our readings from the Bible. We were still best friends more than husband and wife. The birth of Rachel made it more interesting as we brought her into our "fun." Despite the instability, I worried for nothing because we were in the military. We were also in a wonderful and loving church called Calvary Chapel. They enveloped us in the love of Jesus. We both felt like we were part of an incredible church family. It felt like heaven on earth. We were open to doing any volunteer work within the church to further the message of Jesus Christ. I excessively volunteered for any and every ministry I could possibly fulfill. I would even go to people's homes in my church family and clean their houses for them, or I would babysit their children along with mine.

We both also went to hermeneutics Bible studies that taught us seminary level classes on the Bible. We both took to it like fish to water. Originally the classes were only for the men, as our church had very Orthodox Calvinist beliefs. Husbands were expected to teach their wives at home. But I showed a great aptitude for apologetics, and Pastor Marshall made an exception with me as long as I stayed quiet and respectful. This I did during the study. But after the study I had to debate with the other men about the subject matter we just studied. I wanted to know more; I wanted to know all I could. Jacob did, too, and forgot I was his wife and that it was his duty to hush me. So Pastor Marshall seemed to give me a pass. Our debates with each other would get heated and go into the wee hours of the morning. We were on fire for a young couple, and we had everything going for us. Within this church and military life, my agoraphobia could live with me successfully without crippling me completely. I lived in a bubble. It was rare that I had any contact with my neighbors; however, I made some pretty good friendships within the church. Anna, Lana, Cora, and Juniper were my closest friends and dearest sisters. We were kindred spirits. Whereas I went to the Bible study for the men, on Saturday I carried everything I learned there back with me and shared it all with my sisters. Naturally, their husbands had discussed the subject matter with them already. But being able to debate apologetics with them made me stronger as a Christian and a teacher. Eventually word got out that not only was I at the men's Bible study on Saturdays, but that the group of us sisters were becoming well known for having tongues like two-edged swords when it came to the word of God. Pastor Marshall relented and began to let us women attend the men's Saturday Bible study if we stayed respectful and quiet. He did not hold back from reminding all of us of how important it was for the men to teach their wives at home. And how important it was for us women to be respectful towards our husbands and listen quietly beside them so Pastor Marshall could teach them from the word of God how to be more loving towards us. Pastor Marshall never had a problem out of us women during the study time.

Jacob volunteered to serve in Desert Storm. I believe he truly was doing his patriotic duty volunteering. I was tearing up and angry with him for making this choice. He was away for nine months and lived mostly on base, on alert for another ten months. Before he left, I became pregnant with his son Joseph. I carried Joseph by myself while he was away fighting the war. We tried to keep in touch through the wire. There were no cell phones or laptops back then. At one point I cried so hard and deeply during service that Pastor Marshall interrupted the service, walked to the back, and held me tight in his bosom as if I were his child.

While Jacob was gone, I joined a Christian band called Set Free Forever. They needed a third singer for their harmony. Someone suggested I try out and so I did. And I made the cut. This time I did not let my agoraphobia hold me back. With Rachel in tow, I came to every practice and rehearsal and gig that we did. The only trouble I ran into was when it was prayer time after every gig. People would crowd around us on the stage wanting to hold our hands or give us unexpected hugs. I found with the crush of so many people I could not handle it. I said nothing to my bandmates, but they saw how much I was suffering. However, I tried to endure. I did not want to offend anyone. It was part of the ministry. People wanted to come and tell us their life story so we could pray over them or even have the honor of leading them to Christ. When Jacob was beside me, boldness sprung out of me, and I was not afraid of the number of people that might surround us. We made a good evangelistic team. But on my own I had an overwhelming fear that crippled me, and it took all of me to keep from running away. This is what my bandmates saw. Rather than have me suffer and one day someone misunderstand my pain and become offended, we determined halfway through the last song I would leave the stage quietly and go sit on our bus and pray for the team as a whole. This I started doing, and it made the road trips so much easier for all of us. My bandmates did not know I suffered from agoraphobia. They just assumed it had to do with Jacob being gone and my being pregnant.

Jacob came home a changed man. Whatever he saw and lived through, it brought out the violence in him. My gentle giant had died when he stepped on that ship. Someone else came home to me. That evening we had a celebratory dinner in honor of Jacob's homecoming. Now our family was Jacob, me, Rachel, and little Joseph.

When dinner was done, it was an extremely quiet dinner, as Jacob no longer was as talkative and happy as he once was. Jacob said very softly "When we are done here, put the children to bed. I want to make love to my wife."

"Jacob you just got home," I said. "Please, I am not ready yet. It has been over a year since our last time. I am still healing from giving birth to Joseph. Please give me time to prepare myself."

The old Jacob would have smiled and asked me how much time, and we would have debated about how much time was biblically appropriate, eventually settling on a time frame. The new Jacob that came home to me would do no such thing. Jacob quietly got up from the table, walked over behind me, reached for my hair, pulled me off the chair, and dragged me down the hall into the bedroom. By then I was crying and screaming. He let go of my hair in the bedroom, slapped me, walked over to the bed, padded the bed, then sat down and said "Dinner is over. And I want to make love to my wife." Again, I lived in a world of daily abuse. Jacob began to use force, threats, and physical harm to get his way for what he wanted. He would force me to have sex of different kinds I knew nothing about to satisfy himself. The evening times were a time of dread. Instead of what I went through with my dad, now I had my husband almost nightly hitting me or slapping me for something I did wrong, then being dragged or forced into the bedroom for whatever sex situation he would insist on. I had to get used to a large-bodied man lying on top of me all night despite the inability to breathe, let alone sleep.

Jacob removed us from our church and had us canvass other churches to attend. Without the support of my sisters from church or Pastor Marshall and his Bible studies, I would start my day taking diet pills, because I found they would wake me up and give me energy. I needed it from lack of sleep. But hours before Jacob would come home, I would take sleeping pills to help me endure the night and forget all we had lost. After a while there were now four children. Rachel was the first, Joseph was the second, Suzan was the third born out of rape, and Gladys came 11 months apart from her sister, conceived after a horrible fight where I called the police and had Jacob arrested for the first time. He was held for 24 hours, then released. He promptly came home and beat me up properly all over again. It became a habitual ritual to dress my children for bed and lock them in the room away from their father. I did not want them to see or hear anything. Then, when he came home, I would brace myself for "an episode". Many times we went to a church activity after a fight, or even a rape situation. Then we would come back home and it would happen all over again. I do not know how I lived through any of it. Because of the scars and bruises I had, I wore turtlenecks and sweaters, even during the summer, to cover the marks. I always had a reason or a story to tell as for why Jacob was unhappy or why I did not look right. Our first five children were born out of that violence.

Jacob was part of a drug ring in the pharmacy that was caught selling and using pharmaceuticals for monetary reasons. Eight were charged, as well as the commanding officer. They were not able to bring charges against Jacob, who was mostly a mule, so they investigated his home life and charged him with domestic violence, abandonment, and neglect. After ten years of service, he was discharged with a code. He christened the circumstance with his first affair and a refusal to go to work. That night Jacob went missing. I called my parents frantic. Lately since Jacob had come home from the war, he was always falling asleep on himself. He told me he suffered from narcolepsy and petit mal seizures brought on by fighting in the war. I naively believed him. Many nights he did not show up at home from work, and I had to go in search of him. I would call the pharmacy several times looking for him. The guys that worked there with him would joke that Jacob was inebriated somewhere at someone's bar. Or they would joke that he was in the bathroom and could not be awoken. I assumed they joked about Jacob as they did because he was a Christian, and it seemed so odd that he would come home so changed in character with this narcolepsy and petit mal seizure ailment. My father had other ideas. He believed the guys at the pharmacy were telling me what was going on with my husband in the gentlest way possible without coming out and saying he is a drunk and a drug addict. Even if they were telling me that, I probably would not have believed them.

I drove around the base and the city for hours until I saw a figure on the street corner that resembled my husband. It was my husband talking to a street girl. I called out his name and got his attention. He came over to the car and got in.

"Jacob are you alright?" No answer. "Jacob what were you doing. Why were you talking to that woman? Did you have a seizure? Did you get lost? Did you fall asleep on the train? Was it the narcolepsy? Speak to me, Jacob. I do not know what to think."

"What do you think I was doing, Vicky? I had an affair. I paid for sex from a hooker. We had sex all night. I did not do it to hurt you. I just wanted to have sex with someone that wanted it, too."

I started crying at this point.

"Try to understand, Vicki, what it is like to be me married to a wife who does not want me."

"Jacob, I do want you."

"No Vicky, you do not want me; not in the right way. You want me as a friend; a buddy. You do not want me as a husband and a lover. Grownup people are lovers, Vicky."

When we got to my parents' house I ran inside and back into my old room and cried on my bed. I never wanted to leave ever again. I could hear my mom and dad playing with the children in the living room. They truly enjoyed being grandparents. Jacob sat on the couch and said nothing. He just stared at my parents playing with all the little ones wishing that were he and I. After a while, Mom called Jacob and I into her room. She asked me to share with her everything that had happened between Jacob and I since Jacob had gotten home. So I did, letting her know of every detail, every beating, every insult. Then Mom ask Jacob to share his side, starting with when He first got on The Gator Freighter. Jacob refused to share all the details of his time away. He shared about the friends he made, all the countries he went to, and how he became the primary physician when the original one became ill and was sent stateside. That is where Jacob stopped sharing about his time away. He shared his frustration with my unwillingness to have sex with him, and how he had hated himself for a very long time for bullying me into having sex with him. He never mentioned nor acknowledged the beatings, the slapping, the dragging me by the hair, the picking me up and throwing me across the room, or the holding me up in the air by my throat with my feet off the ground watching me choke until I submitted to what he wanted sexually. It was as if he did not know he had done these things, or he was in denial and could not come up front about such heinous behavior in himself. I said nothing. Mom gave us both a long talk throughout the day. She did not want to see us divorce with such beautiful children needing us both. Jacob had lost his Navy career. But he could start again as a pharmacist in a hospital anywhere in the USA. And I was doing very well with my music band. Our tours resulted in a large following. We already had one record out. And our song, *"Colors of the Rainbow"* was Number 5 on the Christian charts. Two producers were courting us. A divorce could mess the whole thing up. Jacob promised to never have an affair again. I promised to go get help from a professional about my sexlessness.

I took on a job driving the transit bus in my area, and I began to run with the fire department as an EMT. I did well, and it was helping me overcome my agoraphobia and the loss of self-esteem because of all the abuse. I began divorce proceedings after Jacob's second affair. I still had not seen a professional. Rather I withheld boldly from my husband, saying I feared if I had sex with him, I would get AIDS since he had been with a whore. Because my parents now knew of the abuse, Jacob was hesitant to hit me, so I became very bold. My anger was so hot, I did not care whether he liked how I dressed, how clean the house was, or whether he liked my dinner. In fact, I stopped putting the kids to bed early. Since he was home feeling sorry for himself, I did not care about anything. All that mattered to me was getting to my job driving the bus on time, spending my time at the fire station running as an EMT, going on tour with my band, and worshipping with now thousands of fans. It was easy to forget how awful life once was when Jacob came home from work. I felt like I was in control of my life now, and no one could tell me what to do.

After Jacob committed his second affair, my parents and I began divorce proceedings, and my father bought a house for me and my children. He and my mom finally learned of all the abuse I was going through with Jacob when he abandoned me while I was pregnant with Gladys. She was supposed to be miscarried. My body was too broken to carry her, and I needed surgery. But I stayed on bed rest for the full nine months at my parents' house and successfully gave birth to her at 32 weeks. She was a preemie miracle. My father tried to use this time to make up for his mistakes by buying me a house if I divorced Jacob. My father was deeply ashamed of Jacob for abusing me and abandoning me and the children as he had done. At first, I agreed. But Jacob came back for me shortly after Gladys's birth and begged my forgiveness, promising things would be better. He would never hurt me again because he needed me. I forgave him and said I would go back. My father was furious.

The praise band I belonged to and toured with at times with was on the verge of a musical contract. Things were looking bright. Then the car accident happened. I had to go to work that evening. So I dropped the children off at Jacob's mom's house. And I headed back up the road toward the fire station. Michael W. Smith was playing on the radio, and I had a bowl of Cool Whip with chocolate chips in it sitting beside me. I was enjoying the sweetness in my mouth and the sweetness of the song in my ears when I was hit head-on at 100 miles an hour by a black van that jumped the median. I was thrown from my seat as my car went under the van that hit me. The floor of the car came up and sandwiched my knees into the dashboard saving my life. My head hit and shattered the windshield, but the dashboard saved my life. The jaws of life found me lying flat with the ceiling of the car inches away from my nose. This is what happened to me. But what I remember is that I woke up and got out of the car and started walking along the side of Route 1. Two women ran towards me and asked me what I was doing.

"I am walking to work," I said.

"You cannot," said one woman who looked like a nurse. "You are hurt, see?" She pointed to my knee which was dislocated.

"How did that happen?" I asked.

"You have been in a terrible car accident," said the other. "You must go back. We must set your leg, or you will lose it."

"OK," I said.

So I went back and sat down on the front seat, while the nurse got behind me and held my head still. The other one bent down, took a hold of my leg, and said, "This is going to hurt, but afterwards you will be OK."

"Alright," I said.

She put my leg back in place. And I screamed and passed out. I opened my eyes and saw a very young and gentle-faced white sheriff staring down at me. He held my hand and told me not to be afraid. I was going to be OK.

"Please do not leave me," I begged.

"I am not going to leave you. I will stay here with you."

I was medevacked to Mary Washington, where I was in a semi-coma for a while. I do not know how long my stay was. My parents are no longer here to remind me. What I do know from my mother's journals is that my husband signed me out against doctors' orders before I woke up. My father and husband thought, from a lawyer's counsel, if my injuries could get worse, they would obtain more money off my circumstance. I remember waking up in my parents' bed and screaming at everyone. But I was screaming inside myself. No one could hear me or even see that I could see and hear everyone around me. I tried to lift my hand unsuccessfully and touch my mother. I did not understand why my parents looked so old. And I didn't recognize who all the children were that stood around the bed. It was a scary time.

My mother was terminally ill with cancer and was bedridden at the time of my accident. My brother Nathan was in the hospital from a car accident a month prior where he had to have reconstructive surgery on his face. His car was hit by a deer that jumped through his windshield in the early morning and smashed him in the face. The only thing that saved his life was a nurse driving behind him. She had the wherewithal to cut a hole in his throat and stick her straw down in it, making it possible for him to breathe. We were both recovering on the same floor and we both had to recover together at our parents' home. My accident motivated my mother to leave her bed and to nurse her children back to health. She lived a year longer than she was supposed to as a result. My father and husband won a half a million-dollar settlement and split it between them. I never saw any of it.

CHAPTER EIGHT

The Monster

Two years after my mother's passing and Jacob divorcing me for his girlfriend, I was working three jobs to care for my five children while still recovering from the car accident. Life was hard. Because of the car accident, our dreams as a band were killed. The band disbanded while I was recovering. Because of my brain injury, I could no longer run with the fire department nor drive a commuter bus. My parents offered to adopt the five children, which would have allowed me to go back to college after I recovered completely, obtained my degree, and began teaching as a teacher, with the hopes of one day becoming a professor. Mom was no longer with us, so Dad was trying to follow through on his promise to Mom to help me succeed. But I did not see it that way. I saw him trying to steal away my children from me because I was now disabled and a failure once more. So I said no, and he said "Fine, you made your bed; now sleep in it."

I met Howard on a blind date, and three months later, we married. I barely knew him, but I wanted to stop working and focus on recovering and on my children. He said he was lonely and wanted company. He told me he was a plumber. He also was the president of our housing community and a foster care parent. I thought I chose well for myself and my children. He seemed like everything I could want in a husband that was an older man. He listened to the same music as I. He enjoyed reading the same Calvinist books as I. He attended the same church as I and liked to dress up in suits like myself. What were the odds of both of us having so much in common? He even dreamed of doing mission work as myself one day. I thought I had found my Prince Charming, and I was very happy. But not everyone.

My father felt Howard was a criminal. My pastor felt Howard was shady and told me so much, but I would not listen. I felt like everyone was being overprotective because I had been injured so badly. I did not like being treated like an invalid, and I let everyone know it. Yes, I survived domestic violence. Yes, I survived rape. Yes, I survived a bad car accident, and now I was living with a traumatic brain injury. But that did not make me a victim or incapable. I wanted to show everyone I was capable of whatever I put my mind to if given the chance. This was my second chance on life. The doctor said socially I had the mind of a seven-year-old, but I wanted to prove I could grow away from that and be a better person. So I did not want anyone's help. I wanted to raise my children myself, and I wanted to work and make my own way myself, despite my disabilities. So I worked myself to the bone with three jobs. When Howard came along, it was as if my Prince Charming had come to relieve me, so all I would need to do is focus on being a mother to my children, without the fear of being beat up or forced to have sex when I didn't want it.

Three months after getting married, my Prince Charming punched me in my mouth and knocked me out.

I awoke in a psychiatric ward tied down to a bed in a quiet room. He had labeled me schizophrenic and told them I was having a psychotic break. I was not, but no one would listen to me. They kept me there against my will for six months highly medicated. I came home highly medicated and constantly sleeping. Howard made sure I took my medication excessively. He would wash it down with alcohol. I had never had alcohol up to this point. My father was an alcoholic, so I had vowed never to have a drink. I saw what it could do, And I did not want to be like my father. But under the influence of the psychiatric drugs, I had no idea what was going on around me. Howard could have fed me dog food, and I would have eaten it gladly. Instead, he fed me higher doses of the psychiatric medication. I was supposed to take it and then wash it down with his alcohol or hard liquor. With such a concoction, most of the time I was asleep or in a daze. It all could have killed me.

No one had any idea what Howard was doing. During the time I was locked up in the psychiatric ward, he was raping my older daughter. She was 11. And being that he had been hired to be the coach on the girls' softball team at our church, he was also raping six other children on the team. All the children He had threatened so that none of them were willing to talk and tell anyone what was happening. The night before the police broke into our house, my daughter Rachel came to me wanting to talk. I was alert enough to see strong concern on her face. "What's wrong, Rachel? Tell me what is wrong." She was quiet for a long time. Howard was already in the bed waiting for me to come. We had a line of pillows that divided his side from mine. In the 14 months we were married, we never consummated our marriage because I was unwilling, and I had stated at the time of our marriage that there would be no sex and he agreed. Rachel could not bring herself to say what was troubling her. I felt maybe she was deeply depressed because she had skipped the fifth grade and went into the sixth grade, because academically she excelled. However, after six weeks, the middle school demoted her back to the fifth grade. They said that socially, she was not ready. For weeks she had been devastated and stayed in her room refusing to come out. I thought finally she was willing to talk about her feelings about being demoted. But she could not bring herself to say anything. I thought maybe it was because she felt she had an audience, since Howard was sitting there in the bed waiting for me. So I said "Well, when you come home from school, Rachel, do you want to talk then?" She nodded her head and agreed, then she walked down the hall to go to bed. She looked back at me, and I her, then she turned the corner. That is all I remember before our world was turned upside down.

The afternoon came when the police broke into my home and arrested Howard. They surrounded my younger children with rifles and waited for the social workers to come and take them away from me. As they dragged the children out the door against their will fighting and screaming, I was held back by the police, fighting and screaming to get to my children myself. Samuel was still nursing and had never been separated from me except when he stayed with Grandma Dorothy while I worked. Now I found myself down in the police department for six hours being interrogated by the investigator. It was like law and order in real life. They got in my face and yelled at me. They accused us of things that were not true just to get at the truth. Pictures were placed in front of me of children I knew, but in inappropriate positions taken by Howard and sold on the black market. At that time, I had never looked at anything rated R. Those images were unbearable. Howard had raped my daughter and seven other children in our community, some in my church. Howard had also broken into people's homes and stole various things for money. He used my home as a cover. The police used my home and family as a stake out to catch him. He had been a criminal for a long time.

I was held for 24 hours, then I was released to go to court and see Howard arraigned. I attempted to go home, but I began to suffer from the chills and shakes. I was sweating all over, and I did not know why. I felt so sick. I passed out on my way to my car. I woke up in the hospital in excruciating pain. They said I had alcohol poisoning, and I was going through withdrawals from being overmedicated. When I went home, I was in complete shock and gave in to full blown alcoholic agoraphobia psychosis for ten months. I lost my mind. I talked, fed, scolded, played with, and loved on my five children as if they were right there in the room with me.

I held and weaned Samuel at 2½ as if he were in my arms with his binky and Blue's Clues cup. I sang to them at night as I tucked them into their beds, and I worked on reading with John as if he were sitting at the table with me. At night, during my witching hour, I wept for the daughter I miscarried and all the hurt and pain I lived through up to that point. I was constantly in a drunken stupor, leaving the house to obtain alcohol and to call on the payphone at the KOA campground. What did I call for? I was in search of my children that had died and wanted to know where the funeral was at. Where had they been buried?

A friend from my church was finally able to come into my home and convinced me to go to dinner with them. His uncle was the landlord of the home I was renting to own before I went mad. Each day he would come into the home, clean up whatever mess I had created, and stock the house with food I never ate, but would cook for my "invisible children," take the garbage out, then "babysit" me for the whole of the day. He even paid my bills. As we drove over the Rappahannock Bridge, I jumped out of the car, and ran to the edge of the bridge and tried to jump. But he and a police officer caught me before I succeeded. I thought I could fly to my children. The officer escorted us to the hospital. There I dried out from alcohol poisoning once more and was sent to a psychiatric center in Richmond to obtain help. I stayed there for three months. In court, the judge sent me home to my father and ordered housing and disability supports for me as well.

Things should have gotten better. The marriage was annulled. We were in my father's home, so I did not have to work. I had a voucher to find a home of our own. But my father had not changed. When I rejected his advances and threats, he kicked me out. As if things could not get even worse, they did. He threatened that if I took the children, He would have me arrested for kidnapping because the children were still in his custody and not mine. Rachel was torn apart as I packed my suitcase to leave.

"Please, Mom, please take me with you. I do not want you to go."

"I cannot take you with me, Rachel. I am going to be staying in a shelter, and I do not know with that is like. If it is anything like TV, then it is dangerous and no place for children. Your grandpa said I cannot stay. I know you do not understand why, and I cannot tell you why. I just cannot stay, And I have no place to go. But you stay here with your siblings and watch over your siblings, and when I get a place for us I will come back for all of you and we will all live together again as a family, OK?"

She cried so pitifully it broke my heart. I did not want to leave, and I was afraid what my leaving might do to her and the others. But I had no choice. I could not do what my father was insisting that I do; it was wrong. Why didn't God come down and do something about the whole matter? Why was He allowing everything to go from bad to worse? I knew God loved me, but I did not understand what God was doing in my life or the life of my children.

I was homeless for the first time. I remember Rachel begging me to take her with me, but I could not. My father could accuse me of kidnapping, as they were not in my care yet. I lived on the street for three days before I got a room in the homeless shelter. Once there I was mugged for my money, and I was molested once again, only by a gang of women in my room. I made several hospital visits as a result to the psychiatric ward. Finally, big Matt moved me to the library room where I would sleep. He allowed me to stay there for seven months.

Once I obtained a home for us, my children would stay with me by day. I would go to the vocational center while they were in school. It was court-ordered as an attempt to help me overcome agoraphobia. But my children and I were broken. There was an unsettling sadness in our home. I did not know how to parent them anymore. I did not know how to care for myself. We tried to find solace and peace in the church and in music. I was new to sobriety and used church to stay dry, but I was continually reminded of my failures as a parent and as a human being.

CHAPTER NINE

Our True Heart

Let us take a break and deviate a little bit. I think it is important to explain something in detail before we go on. As human beings, every aspect of us is connected: the spiritual, the physical, and the mental. Each part affects the other and determines our choices and our decisions. Every sin we commit, every sacrifice we make for others, every successful event, and every failure has a real-life effect on us, and on those around us. Those effects can lengthen our lives or shorten them. Those effects can strengthen our faith or crush it.

I wrote this chapter two years before I wrote Chapter 1, and I wrote it for a class project while in school. Only reading it now did I realize how vital this chapter is to the book. Our hearts are at the center of our choices, decisions, hopes, pain, despair, loss, sin, anger and the very life force that gives us breath. When the beat of our heart discontinues, so does all life. I have often wondered why my heart did not stop beating even when I had died. Maybe this chapter can explain. Your heart determines what you believe, what you think, what you worship, and what you fear. We give lip service constantly because we want others to believe things about ourselves that may not be true. We want them to think we are a good person, a smart person, someone who can be trusted, someone who can be looked up to. But our hearts will always give us away. In the end, we are how we live.

Most of us take our hearts for granted. It is that fragile/tough little red muscle inside our chest that constantly pumps blood, oxygen, and water back and forth throughout our body, motivated by electrical current so that we might live. For it to do its job at the most optimum, we must feed it good foods like fruits and vegetables, good starches like rice and potatoes, healthy meats, tons of crystal clean water, and soothing milks like nuts, cow's milk, and yogurts. Our hearts also feed off the amount of sleep we give them, the amount of exercise we indulge in, and the wonderful air we choose to breathe. If we are vigilant in doing all this, as well as keeping our stress level to a minimum, our hearts can keep us alive and dancing like a young person for many years to come.

Let us apply this scenario to our spiritual heart, our emotional heart, and our mental heart. What foods do we need to feed these hearts of ours for them to perform at their best? How much rest and oxygen do these hearts need? What kind of water do they thirst for? What is their motivator and how much stress level is over the top for these hearts? Have you ever considered that you have a spiritual heart, an emotional heart, and a mental heart? Are you caring for your spiritual heart and emotional heart as much as you care for your physical heart? And who gives these hearts a checkup? Let's explore a little more with our physical heart, and from there, we can dissect each other's hearts to get a clearer understanding of their functional needs and what we can do to strengthen and mend each one when they become sick.

There are two parts to our heart, the left and the right, divided by a muscle in between them. It consists of an upper and lower chamber, and the chambers are connected by valves that the blood flows through. The heart pumps, sending electrical currents through each chamber, each side doing a specific job to keep the body functioning. The right side pumps oxygen-rich blood to the lungs, and the left side cleans the blood that enters it so the body can be healthy. One side receives and then cleans the blood; the other side oxygenates the blood, so as it flows out through the coronary arteries, the body functions at optimum with blood, water, and oxygen clean and ready to make the body powerful. Information along these lines can be accessed through the following links: https://www.heartfoundation.org.au https://www. heartfoundation.org.au/your-heart/.

Much of the following information was obtained from an Internet article entitled "Human Heart: Anatomy, Function & Facts" by Tanya Lewis, and it is available on the website www.livescience.com. The graphics in this chapter were also obtained from that article.

The heart pumps blood through the circulatory system, which supplies the body with oxygen-rich nutrients, removing carbon dioxide and waste.

This small instrument, the size of one's fist, formed by God, when all the details are stripped away, comes down to plumbing, electricity, and structure. There is a specific order, and there are specific guidelines and specific rules that the motor (heart) must follow to run and to make the body function adequately. I could go on into more detail, and I will, but it is clear: there is nothing simple about this muscle, and yet, there is everything serendipitous about it. So, it is with our souls.

Let us dig a little deeper. Our heart has four chambers: the atria on top and the ventricles below on both the left and right sides. The septum separates the two sides. The pericardium encases our heart, protecting it and anchoring it to the chest in the body. Our soul consists of our emotional self and our mental agility. It is separated by our spiritual wall and encased in our will, which anchors us to the chest of life.

If we look further, we find that the encasement has three layers: the epicardium which holds our blood, the pericardium which is on the outside, and the myocardium which is in the middle and contracts. The valves connecting the atria and ventricle chambers are called atrioventricular valves. The heart strings connect the valves to the heart muscle. Break the heart strings and the result is loss of circulation through the pulmonary oxygenated circuit pathway and the systemic (blood cleansing) circuit pathway, creating eventual death. We want to take care of our heart strings to keep the system working. Such fragile things, the heart strings, are responsible for such an important system, these two circuits. How does this work?

In the pulmonary pathways, oxygen-rich blood goes from the right chamber to the lungs, then to the left chamber through the pulmonary veins. The systemic pathway with oxygen-rich blood goes through the left chamber, through arteries and capillaries feeding the tissue with oxygen. Then the deoxygenated blood comes back through the right chambers. Without oxygen and nutrients, the heart would quickly die, and all systems would end abruptly.

We function on the breath of God flowing through us and the food he daily feeds us. Whether we know it or acknowledge it, it is His grace and his mercy that is our air and our food. He is our cardiovascular system pumping blood (His love) through our hearts, to our lungs, and all around our body. But it is our will that can block God's grace and mercy from strengthening our soul and leading us closer to Him and to His love. We can create a blockage within our valves that can lead to a stroke or, worse, a heart attack damaging the muscle (our spirit) that divides the chambers (our emotions and our thoughts or mind) and leading to the weakening of the wall (our will) that encases our heart. That blockage could be any amount of sin in our lives; whether our thoughts, our words, or our actions, it hinders movement, health, stability, and maturity. The electrical currents are then affected, disturbing the rhythm of the heartbeat. This disturbance leads to cardiac arrest. Cardiac arrest is the sudden stop of the rhythm and the death of the heart. What once was alive now becomes dead. This small, fragile, complicated instrument moves and turns this intricate machine called man. Yet one sin, one wound, one unresolved problem over time can block the flow of God's love throughout the body, putting a cease-and-desist sign up in front of grace and mercy, exposing the vulnerable heart strings and causing them to detach, and interrupting the electrical current of God's power in one's life, resulting in sudden heart attack that could easily lead to cardiac arrest and death.

Let us look at one more detail about this little red muscle. God knows how easy it is for the valves to become blocked. The blood (His love) washes nutrients in and throughout the body, but it also carries away waste that must be cleaned away. This waste, our sins, causes blockages if allowed to build up over time. So, God, in His infinite wisdom, put electrical pacemaker cells in the blood that produces our heartbeat. This is God's backup plan to our fleshly weakness. Every cell could lead, and all the others follow. But everyone cannot be the leader. Who would follow? The rhythm would end up being off. So, God gives them all an opportunity to lead in time in five stages, all of them working together.

God's love, as he washes our sins away, leads us repeatedly to repentance, and God is more than happy to forgive. He continually gives us ample opportunity to repent and to clean ourselves up through the cleansing blood of His love. In the first stage, the heart relaxes. We must humble ourselves before our Father.

As the atrium contracts, pushing blood into the ventricle, it continues, then empties and relaxes again. As we fall on our faces before God and pour out the contents of our heart at the feet of God, He washes over us, He cleanses us, He renews us through the passion of His love for us, and He fills us with His hope. The sins we held onto emptied out of us as we repented before the forgiving face of God.

Can you hear the symphony of your heart? Every beat is a cadence of clean blood flowing out and blood that needs washing flowing in. In the same, the orchestra of constant repenting of our sins flows into the heart of God, becoming washed away, and out flows his love through us repeatedly. The cycle keeps repeating itself as long as the body lives. Prayer, repentance, and forgiveness make up the rhythm and music that beats through our soul as we allow His grace and mercy to feed us; His love continues to flow through valves and in and out of each chamber that makes me. Can you see it? And do not worry about backflow; I know what you engineers are thinking. God has that covered too. His love (our blood) flows in only one direction through our hearts: to the truth. Only our holding onto sin can cause backflow, which results in heart weakness.

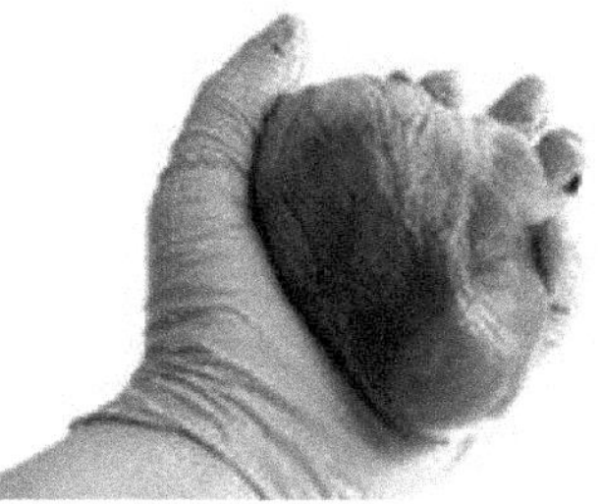

Now understanding this about our physical heart and all its functions, let us look at our soul's heart and make some comparisons. I am going to paint for you another picture of three hearts that function as one. They are the emotional heart, the mental heart, and the spiritual heart. They are encased within the physical heart metaphorically and are tied together by our will within our mind.

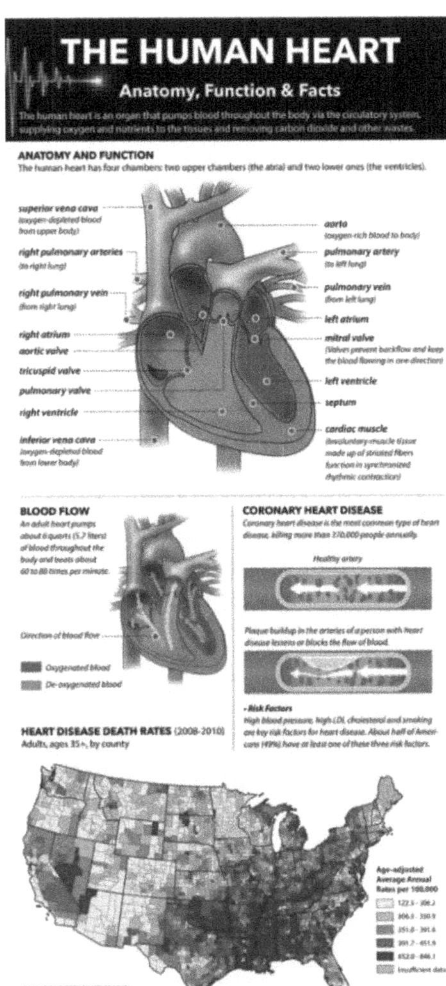

THE HUMAN HEART
Anatomy, Function & Facts
The human heart is an organ that pumps blood throughout the body via the circulatory system, supplying oxygen and nutrients to the tissues and removing carbon dioxide and other wastes.

ANATOMY AND FUNCTION
The human heart has four chambers: two upper chambers (the atria) and two lower ones (the ventricles).

superior vena cava
(oxygen-depleted blood from upper body)
right pulmonary arteries
(to right lung)
right pulmonary vein
(from right lung)
right atrium
aortic valve
tricuspid valve
pulmonary valve
right ventricle
inferior vena cava
(oxygen-depleted blood from lower body)

aorta
(oxygen-rich blood to body)
pulmonary artery
(to left lung)
pulmonary vein
(from left lung)
left atrium
mitral valve
(Valves prevent backflow and keep the blood flowing in one direction)
left ventricle
septum
cardiac muscle
(Involuntary muscle tissue made up of striated fibers function in synchronized rhythmic contraction)

BLOOD FLOW
An adult heart pumps about 6 quarts (5.7 liters) of blood throughout the body and beats about 60 to 80 times per minute.

Direction of blood flow
Oxygenated blood
De-oxygenated blood

CORONARY HEART DISEASE
Coronary heart disease is the most common type of heart disease, killing more than 370,000 people annually.

Healthy artery

Plaque buildup in the arteries of a person with heart disease lessens or blocks the flow of blood.

- Risk Factors
High blood pressure, high LDL cholesterol and smoking are key risk factors for heart disease. About half of Americans (49%) have at least one of these three risk factors.

HEART DISEASE DEATH RATES (2008-2010)
Adults, ages 35+, by county

Age-adjusted Average Annual Rates per 100,000
122.5 - 306.2
306.3 - 350.9
351.0 - 391.6
391.7 - 451.9
452.0 - 846.1
Insufficient data

Alaska
Hawaii

Rates are spatially smoothed to enhance the stability of rates in counties with small populations.
Data Source: National Vital Statistics System, National Center for Health Statistics

SOURCES: National Center for Chronic Disease Prevention and Health Promotion, Division for Heart Disease and Stroke Prevention, LiveScience.com
R. TORO / © LiveScience.com

livescience

They function in symbiosis with each other, and if the physical heart is sick, the other hearts will be sick too. If the spiritual or emotional or the mental heart becomes sick, so do the other hearts as well. So, let us look at it in this regard: the physical heart has two sides, the left muscle and the right muscle. But our overall heart has four functioning muscles: the spiritual muscle of the heart, which is on top or north; the emotional muscle of the heart, which is second or due west; the mental muscle of the heart, which is third or due east; and the physical muscle of the heart, which is fourth or due south. So it may look like this:

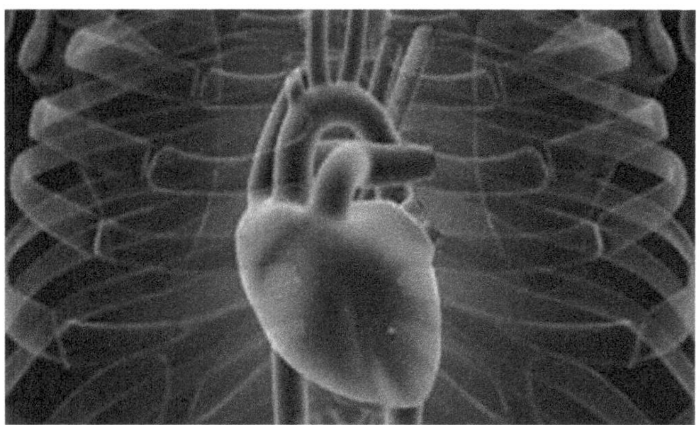

For each part of our true heart there is a muscular wall that keeps them separate from each other and pumps the life force throughout them. That muscular wall represents our thoughts, our needs, and our wants. Throughout our true heart there are valves that connect these muscles together in which blood flows throughout.

Those connective valves carry our wants, thoughts, and needs throughout these four muscles within the life force. The pumping of the heart muscle is controlled by ventricles which carry electrical currents to the heart muscle and keep it massaged so that it pumps continuously. With our true heart, it is our spirit that carries the electrical currents of life to our true heart muscle, massaging it and causing it to pump at the optimum rate needed for healthy life.

Now in the physical heart, the right muscle pumps oxygen to the lungs so that we may breathe at our healthiest. In our true heart, the mental muscle pumps oxygen to our lungs so that we might breathe at our best. The mental muscle is the second muscle or due east. That muscle, as it is pumping the best oxygen to the body, it massages the emotional muscle of the heart, blanketing it with the oxygen it needs to function well and be healthy too. The spiritual muscle of the heart, which is due north and connected to all the other heart muscles, first extends its oxygen to the mental muscle, which then massages the emotional muscle, which then extends that oxygen to the physical muscle. Now the blood, which is the life force of our hearts, is pumped by the left physical heart muscle into the right muscle and then throughout the body.

Within our diagram, the blood (the hope inside of us) is pumped from the mental muscle into the emotional muscle and down to the physical muscle. This hope blood is formed in the spiritual heart muscle and begins its journey from the spiritual heart muscle to the mental heart muscle, then into the emotional heart muscle and down to the physical heart muscle.

All these workings are happening simultaneously and consistently. All this blood and oxygen is spread out throughout the heart muscle and then throughout the body through coronary arteries, and then the circulatory system. This system supplies blood, oxygen, and nutrients to the body. It also removes carbon dioxide and waste from the body.

Similarly, our hope carries our life spirit, which is the oxygen, the light of our hope, which includes the blood and the necessities of our soul, which are the nutrients going throughout our heart and then into the body so we can function properly. The waste of hopelessness, apathy, and all other negative thoughts, ideas, desires, and sins (carbon dioxide) are carried out of the body as waste and disposed of. Our soul (the heart) needs a constant supply of nutrients just as the tissue of the body needs a constant source of nutrients. If the blood (the word of God or whatever scripture we feed through our body) does not supply the soul with what it needs, the soul will slowly die, just as the tissue of the body will slowly die.

The physical heart is basically structure, electricity, and plumbing. The true heart is basically the four parts (structure), powered by our spirit (electricity), and cleansed through our hope (plumbing). A double walled sac called the pericardium encircles and encases the heart, protecting it and keeping it rooted to the chest. The sac in which our true heart sits in is the force that keeps us alive (Father God). It is our will, and it protects our true heart and keeps it anchored to the chest of the body. The stronger our will, the tougher our protective sac around our true heart and the deeper the roots go, keeping it secure.

In the circulatory system of the heart, we have deoxygenated blood that leaves through the right heart ventricle via the artery to the lungs, and we have oxygenated blood that returns and enters the left atrium via the pulmonary veins. In our true heart, the life force that is contaminated goes out through the mental muscle to be cleaned, and the life force that is full of our spirit (oxygenated blood) comes in through our emotional heart muscle. If there is a blockage of any kind, and the contaminated blood cannot get to the right muscle, or the spirit-enriched blood cannot get to the left muscle, just as the physical heart can have a heart attack, so can the true heart have a heart attack too. This is where we feel the excruciating pain and crush of deep depression, the symptomatic reactions of mental illness and emotional disturbances, the life-threatening flashbacks of Post Traumatic Stress Disorder (PTSD), and the sickly succumbing to suicidal and even homicidal ideations.

A disturbance in the electrical workings of the physical heart is a cardiac arrest, which is different than a heart attack. A cardiac arrest can lead to a heart attack, but it is not the same. There are "pacemaker cells" (God's word) within the heart that are electrically charged and stimulate the pumping of the heart. When there is a disturbance to the electric charges of these cells, you have a cardiac arrest.

Similarly, with the true heart, if there is a disturbance to the electric current in our true heart—that electric current being our spirit—our true heart will cease to function, and cardiac arrest will ensue. Our spirit must charge the four muscles of our true heart continuously, regularly, and with a consistent rhythm for life to continue flowing and for function not to cease. If our spirit is being flooded with hopelessness, apathy, regret, and sorrow, the charge will become weak or even stop. The myth of the broken heart is just this. The grief of loss is so great, and the pain of sorrow and despair is so heavy and overwhelming, that the electrical charge of our spirit is snuffed out. As a result, cardiac arrest happens, leading to a heart attack, and the body begins to die.

Are you beginning to see how the physical, mental, emotional, and spiritual hearts are all tied to each other? I took my physical heart for granted and pushed it beyond its limits. I took my treasures, my children's hearts, for granted and broke them more than they already were—abandoning them to my fears, my pain, my sorrow, the past. I took my emotional heart for granted and I let my true self die, attempting to protect the true me against an angry, awful world. I put my spiritual heart to death, because I could not believe that a loving God would allow so much ugliness and pain in the life of anyone, and I came to accept that I was cursed and that there was no way around it. I was persuaded that God had no intentions to bless me or restore my life. I was dead, and I believed that I deserved all the bad that had come to me and would continue to come to me, because I could not protect my children or meet God's impossible standards. I took my heart for granted, and eventually I would break it.

I believed these lies so strongly, I lived them out, blinded to the truth that was ever before me: God had not abandoned me; I abandoned Him. God had never stopped loving me from the day I was born; I stopped believing in His love, and I threw myself into a journey through the wilderness without fellowship with my Father. God never cursed me; I lived as if I were cursed because I refused God's blessings repeatedly. God's care and protection was not limited because bad things happened to me or around me; I refused to trust God and obey His will because I feared men around me and chose to place my faith in others. God is a jealous God. He is jealous for our love and devotion towards Him. He is not willing to share it with any demigod, because no one is capable or able to love me as deeply as the Creator of the universe. The Almighty God will go to all lengths to bring the truth out about the deceiver and His minions. Our Loving Father does not want us deceived following a lie. Though the truth is hidden in the dark, God shines His light and exposes the truth every time, so the way is made clear for us to repent and return to the lover of our souls.

CHAPTER TEN

Forever Cursed

By this time, I was going through the motions of living. I had joint custody of my children with my dad. I was court-ordered to go to the vocational center and to have case management through the Community Services Board (CSB). I had to prove I was a good parent, prove I was a good person, prove I was a good Christian, and prove I was a good daughter. When I went to the vocational center, I would sit apart from others in a room or in a corner to myself and watch the life go by. At the church I attended, I sat in the foyer and listened to the service over the speakers by myself. If I sang in the choir, I sat by myself in the choir loft and stayed to myself. The church gave me a job at their preschool, and I isolated there as much as I could. When I was home with my children, I tried to reconnect with them, but my father would often come earlier than he was supposed to in order to take them away from me again.

I spent many nights crying, missing my children. But eventually, I began to distance myself from my children as well. When I failed, or made mistakes, I was my worst judge. I harshly came down on myself, inside my head. When someone else chimed in (usually one of the older ladies from my church), I quickly agreed and beat myself up with whatever observation that person made of me. I had deeply sinned against God. I broke His commands. I dishonored my Father's name. I did not deserve His forgiveness. My daughter got hurt because of my lack of protection and attention to who Howard was. She got hurt because I was tired of my life. I did not deserve His forgiveness. I was cursed. His blessings were removed from me. I was cursed. I could no longer open my Bible or pray. I could not sit with God's people for fear of being attacked by someone that saw the coverage in the paper. I was still haunted by the bad dreams of the elders meeting with me and escorting me out of their church telling me people did not feel comfortable with me being there. I could still feel the woman who came up to me on the street and pointed at me, "You're the woman who let that monster hurt the children," and she spit in my face. Or the woman, during service, who turned around and said, "Are you that lady?" I just smiled.

"What are you doing here?" She whispered. "Why are the children still with you?"

Many mornings I woke up in sweat shivering from the fear of going out the front door. Since I could not drink anymore, the only thing I knew to do to keep my sanity was to just stay busy, keep moving forward, and act as if the past never was. I started volunteering for anything and everything that I could. I would watch TV shows with my kids to totally erase the life that was. I began to come out of my shell and associate with people, as Mr. Willie began to use me to teach workshops at the vocational center. Later, he sent me for training as a Wellness Recovery Action Plan (WRAP) facilitator and then as a Peer Support Specialist.

I began to date various gentleman, not because I was attracted to them or was interested in sex, but because it allowed me to forget the life that once was. I put my attention into the person I was dating instead of facing myself and my life.

First, I dated Ken. Ken was the one who was driving me over the Rappahannock Bridge when I dropped out of the car and tried to jump off the bridge. Next I dated Elisha. He was quiet and steady. But I eventually learned he was 30 years older than me, so I ended it after a year. Then, I began to date Gary, who seemed so much like me, an intellectual, but unlike me, he was rough and dirty and could be foul. I liked being with him because our conversation could be intense. Too intense. The arguing eventually became too much, and I broke it off. But I missed him more than I should have. The next was John. John was in a wheelchair because of cerebral palsy. However, he was extremely charming with a shiny penny smile. I enjoyed being with John, but I had to end this relationship too because he smoked and sold marijuana. That just was not my thing. Then Ken reentered my life. He still lived in Stafford and we still talked on the phone on occasion, but then he would come and stay at my house for several weeks at a time. I liked his company because he was familiar, safe, and I was not alone. Aloneness made me face the past again. I was running hard away from the past.

My father and my church did not like the stream of men and friends from the vocation center going through my house daily. They questioned whether any of them were safe, or whether I was putting my children in danger again. My father made it hard for me to be with my children, constantly taking them away as soon as he had dropped them off. His excuse was the friends I kept. Church friends would refuse to come to my home or have me come to their home, complaining that they felt uncomfortable with the friends that I kept from the vocational center. I became frustrated. I could not be alone. My witching hour would swallow me up. The crying was becoming a physical pain, and my desire to drink was hounding me. But having people distrust me, question my integrity, or see me as unfaithful or reckless was too much.

Never again did I want to make the same mistake as being a neglectful mother because I made another bad choice in people. So, I made some hard choices. I stopped having my vocational friends over at my house. I made a business agreement with Ken, then he and I eloped on St. Patrick's Day 2006. For four months, no one knew we were married. And then I took my father to court and sued him for full custody of my children back. In court, he and other witnesses made me out to be a monster, the first day of court, as if I had committed Howard's crime on my daughter. I was devastated and broken. The second day of court, my lawyer went after my father and brothers like a lion, bringing up the past abuse of my father on our family and the recent abuse toward my son Joseph. The final blow was when he brought up the abuse towards myself at my father's hand. My father was speechless. He shot me a look of deep contempt. We were all sworn to secrecy. This was to never be spoken of and yet, here it was, in all its ugly nastiness, laid out in the light. My father could not get away. My brothers looked at me with disgust after the court hearing was over. The judge ruled that my children were to be removed from my father's care immediately, and I was given full custody. Dad was given supervised visitation as a grandparent. The kids were no longer allowed to be at his house. I would learn years later that my father went home and disowned me from his will permanently. He put Rachel in my place, as if she were his daughter and I never was.

Life with Ken was not easy. Ken was bipolar. He was a classic bipolar. You did not know when he would be going through his highs. But when he did, life became unbearable and full of drama. Then he would crash and begin his depression, which would come dark and grey. His cycles were hopelessly without end, and when he was off his medication (which was most of the time), he was out of control. From gambling away his disability check and work money to being unable to get out of bed and out of the house to go to work because of his depression, I was left on my own. I fussed and screamed continuously at him, with no positive results for him or me. I had the same no-sex agreement with him like everyone else. But this time I was mean about it. Ken was not allowed in my bed. I made him sleep on the floor or the couch or the lazy boy, but never in my bed. I refused to fix big dinners for him.

He had to clean His own clothes and hang them up. And when he threatened to hit me because I disrespected him so unlovingly before the children, I grabbed the butcher knife and put it to his throat and threatened to cut it if he ever laid a finger on me.

Finally, Ken and I struck an agreement. Before any of us were able to begin as a family again, we lost custody of Joseph. Joseph was my autistic baby. He was born delayed because the umbilical cord had been wrapped tightly around his neck. He was not breathing for a long time, so he suffered brain damage. He started walking at the age of five and started talking by the age of seven. Joseph was not able to read until the fourth grade and had gone to special school all his life. By the time he was a preteen, he was a big boy and very tall, but he had the mind of a 9-year-old and did not know his strength. When he got angry, he would throw his toys at people, not recognizing he could hurt someone. Twice he had already pushed me down the stairs. I said nothing so he would not get hurt, but by the second time my father insisted that Joseph come stay with him so that he would not hurt me. Even though we had the judge's decision in effect, I thought it wise to let Joseph stay with my dad. Unfortunately, during that time, he had been breaking the law by stealing at the local 7-Eleven. I had a local police officer take him aside in his car and have a strong talk with him.

Before the dust could settle, Gladys came to me and told me she wanted to hurt herself. Her brother had been hurting her and she wanted it to stop. My heart dropped into my stomach. How was I supposed to handle this? At their grandfather's house, Joseph would come into his sister's room and touch her inappropriately and against her will. The next morning, I got my children up and dressed. I gave them breakfast, then loaded up the car and took everyone over to the family counselor, Mrs. Nutella. I let Gladys share with Mrs. Nutella what had happened to her. Mrs. Nutella took me aside and informed me that either she would have to call the police or me. I did not want another circumstance of me being found negligent in my care of the kids again. I chose to call the police myself. They encouraged me to bring him to the Garfield station. I left the other children with Mrs. Nutella and brought Joseph over to Garfield. I watched them handcuff my boy and take hm away from me like a criminal. My heart was broken that day.

We went to court a while later, and I requested to meet with the judge and prosecutor in the judge's chambers. Gladys was shaking over the idea of taking the stand. She looked so fragile, and she was very frightened. Even though I was not allowed to see my son, I knew he was just as fragile and frightened as his sister. He was only fourteen. She was only ten. I spent five hours in the judge's chambers arguing on behalf of both my daughter and my son. The prosecutor was confused. He expected me to give my son up, to be angry at him, to want them to throw the book at him. Instead I was pleading for him to receive mercy and I pleaded for compassion for Gladys just as strongly.

"How could you plead for him?" the prosecutor asked.

"He is my son, and she is my daughter," I argued. "I love them both the same, and they both need me. They both need help. Prison won't help him, and if she takes the stand, it won't help her."

The judge heard me. He removed Joseph from our home and sent him to his dad on probation until he turned 18. Gladys did not have to take the stand, but she did have to go get help, especially since she threatened suicide.

Ken and I had a written agreement before we married. Some of the things we agreed to included no smoking, no yelling, and no sex. I still naively believed I could convince a man to be with me without sex. Ken was desperate not to be homeless, and he was infatuated with me. He wanted to spend his life with me, and he wanted someone to take care of him. I was agreeing to do just that; just agree to my childish terms. So he did. But, from the beginning, he broke the "no smoking" agreement, and I broke the "no yelling" agreement. The games were on. Four months into our marriage, Ken's heart gave out in my living room. I watched his eyes roll back into the back of his head while we watched TV together. At the emergency room, as they were admitting him into ICU, his doctor chewed me out royally for not knowing his medication routine and making sure he was regularly taking it. I was devastated and humiliated. How could I say I was his wife and not know all the medications he had to take? He was released after 12 days. As soon as he walked out the hospital, he asked for a cigarette from a passerby. My Ken.

The next agreement to go was sex. For months he chased me and begged me, but I refused. Then he hit me to my heart: "Don't you miss Rachel and Joseph?" That question always stopped me yelling cold in my tracks. The tears would roll, and for a while I would be lost to despair. For a while he persuaded me by disarming me with my guilt and longing.

We finally came to a new agreement: We would have sex until I became pregnant with a son, then that would be it. That specific night, we prayed together, holding the Bible and asking God to honor us with a son to take the place of the children I had lost. "Give me a chance to do things right all over again," I prayed. That night we conceived Anna. I was ecstatic.

For a time, my church family, my co-workers at my job, the children at home, Ken, and those at the Vocational Center were all excited and glad for the coming of my daughter. Everything seemed so bright and happy during that time. I remember coming to church and telling my hero, Gabriel, the good news. He took hold of my hand and he looked at me proudly with tears in his eyes. He held my hand for a long time. You would have thought he was the father.

During this time, I had my biography given to an author; I was one among several hundred others. My story among six others was selected to be part of a book called *Firewalkers*. We were all sent away on a retreat for about a week. During this time, the author interviewed each of us wanting to know our stories in detail so she could share with the world in her book. During this time, I had also begun working a job as a life coach. I would counsel people from all walks of life who were learning for the first time how to live with their disabilities or how to come to terms with the end of their lives. I also taught workshops for groups about hope and recovery. As I was growing as a Christian, I was learning just how much God truly loved me and how precious I was to him. And despite my disabilities and shortcomings, I realized he could still use me. I was also learning a lot about forgiveness. Shortly after Howard had gone to jail and after I had a home for my children and I, my father called me on the phone. Dad asked me to come to his house. He said Jacob was there and wanted to talk to me.

"Dad, I cannot come there; you know that," I said. "There is a court order. Jacob's not allowed to be around me."

"Do not be afraid, Vicki," Dad said. "I will be right here, and he assured me he has no intentions of hurting you. He just wants to talk. It is important."

I drove over to my father's house. And I brought Ken with me just to be safe. When I came in, Jacob admitted sincerely and humbly that he had been wrong. He should never have divorced me. He said life did not get better for him, and when he saw his children during visitation, he realized what a great mistake he had made. He should have stayed and helped me through my recovery, he said. He should have been more patient with me and got me help for my problem rather than forcing himself on me. He should not have abused me. Had he not, we would still be in the military today, and had he not, we would still be a family. He realized that he had made some grave mistakes and that he could not take any of it back. All he knew he could do was to ask me to forgive him for all that he had done. I was stunned and amazed that here he stood asking me to forgive him for the worst things that he had done. He did not hold back from admitting his faults. I shook his hand. And I told him I forgave him even though we could never be friends again. He accepted that, and we ended up hugging each other.

Shortly after the book was published and we were touring around doing book signings and speaking engagements, I received a knock on my door. A producer of documentaries wanted to interview me for a documentary called *Hope and Recovery*. I had more speaking engagements, and I even was a master of ceremonies for one of the mental health awareness days.

Ken came to me wanting to have sex again. By this time, he was working his own job in telemarketing. With me busy with *Firewalkers* speaking engagements and WRAP workshops and him with his job, we seemed to be doing okay. But Ken wanted to be together and I did not. I was not very kind. I would make him sleep on the couch, the floor, or a chair. But I would not let him sleep with me in our bed. Ken began to get mean and threatening. I was fearful I was making him like Jacob—abusive. I had too much good happening for Ken and me to have a falling out. So, we struck a new agreement. We would have sex again until I conceived a son, then no more.

That January I sat in the bathroom, me and God, and we had a long talk. I had always wanted to own my own home instead of being on Section 8. With everything going so well, money saved up from the Social Security Disability Insurance (SSDI) bonus, and the money I got from Jacob's unpaid child support, I felt like I was ready to put another down payment on a home of our own. But I was talking about having another baby with Ken.

Doing both would be difficult and complicated. I might fail. I couldn't afford to fail again. But then, everything was going well. Maybe God had forgiven me and now all of heaven had finally opened, and all the blessings of God were now pouring out on me. Which way should I go? We had no more room in the two-bedroom apartment, but now I was introducing a new baby. That would be seven of us in a two-bedroom? However, if I didn't agree to do this "sex" thing, Ken would leave, making me look really bad. Or worse, he might try to force me, like Jacob did, and that would mess me up in my head again. I couldn't afford to get messed up in my head again. The kids needed me; the people I was reaching about hope in recovery needed me. I could not become unhinged again.

This time, conception took time. By February 2009, I was pregnant with my Emmanuel. This time, no one was happy with my conception. No one celebrated. The kids grew silent and distant. Ken and I argued daily; sometimes things got physical. I gave up the apartment and put my money down on a home through Gabriel. We ended up going to a shelter for housing. I assumed it would be temporary, and I tried to pretend like we were on vacation. I placed my money in the hands of the one person I trusted more than anyone else in the world. That was Gabriel.

When I finally found a home for me and my children, and I was no longer living in the shelter, I started going to Gabriel's church. It was such a joy today to see Gabriel once again. He was my Superman, my archangel. After all these years I still looked up to him as I did when I was 16 and he was 21. When I came to church on Sunday, I felt safe when I saw Gabriel there. When I sang with the choir and Gabriel led the choir on the piano, I felt safe because Gabriel was there. And even though I could not sit in the sanctuary with the congregation but sat in the foyer for service, I still felt safe because Gabriel was there. Sometimes I would even visit him at his job and bring him lunch as a way of saying, "Thank you for being you, my Superman." I know it sounds very childish, but I felt everything was coming together, and Gabriel was playing a big part in that, because as long as he was there, I was safe from any of the harm that I endured in the past. And he was also playing a part as a role model to my kids as they grew up, so I felt safe. In fact, I put a lot of trust in Gabriel more than I did in God. And with the pursuit of this house, I completely trusted Gabriel to follow through and make it happen. So staying in a shelter for two weeks with my kids did not trouble me.

But Gabriel came back to me and told me the bank went under and our money was lost. I made myself homeless.

My heart sank, and despair set in among the kids. I was a failure once more. I failed to protect my family again. I did not plan well, and now all the money I had was gone. We were homeless as a family because of me. Gabriel offered to let Gladys, Suzan, and Samuel live with him, while Ken and I figured out our housing. Being at the shelter, my agoraphobia set in like a vengeance, and I refused to go out into the common area or eat with others. I spent most of my time in my room. Ken could not stand being kept in the room with a crying baby and a fussy wife. I am sure during this time he turned back to drugs and some unfaithfulness, but I have no evidence. Only a feeling. When our thirty days were up, we went to a hotel and stayed there. I began to use what money I had left to pay for our weekly stay. The arguing between Ken and me turned to daily fighting, and the kids could not stomach it anymore. I was so caught up in fighting with Ken, I did not see I was slowly losing my children. Gabriel came to their rescue and began to replace me as their parent, sowing seeds of contempt for my authority and love for his fathering in them. Others came to their rescue as well. I was oblivious to what was going on in the lives of my children because I was so focused on my failure to provide us a forever home and the cyclic issues surrounding Ken's bipolar disorder.

At one of my workshops that I taught at, one of my participants assumed I was living comfortably in the suburbs because of the way I dressed and carried myself, and he assumed I had no idea what the plight of their addiction and homelessness was like. "Why are you smiling?" he chided me. "There is no reason to be happy so stop smiling. We are frigging homeless. We have nothing. There is no reason to be happy. You would not understand."

Before this happened, I usually had a speech thoroughly written out. I was prepared chock full of facts about why disabled people should have hope about life. It was usually the generic stuff. You know, be thankful that you can breathe, that you can walk, that if you have hands you can use them, that if you still have eyes you can see, or if you have ears you can hear, find gratefulness deep inside yourself, and learn to be grateful for the things that you do have and that you are still able to do. But this situation was a fork in the road for me. He was right; what was there to be happy about? I was homeless, too, and I could not find anything to be happy about. But none of them knew that, not even my coworkers. Everyone assumed that I was comfortably snuggling down in a home with my five children and that I had a wonderful relationship with my two adult children. This was far from the truth. It was time to tell the truth.

"You are right, Mr. Epstein," I said. "There is no reason to be happy when you are homeless. And I know all about that. I was once homeless before for seven months because I refused to sleep with my father when he insisted that I do. So he kicked me out. And I know all about homelessness now, because I am living in a shelter right now. I lost my home because of my own bad judgment, and I do not know what I am going to do just like you. And you know what? I want to have a drink again, too. But I can't, because I made a promise to the judge that if he gave me my children back, I would never drink again. Because once I was an alcoholic. So, in these next eight weeks, why don't we all work together hard to obtain our forever homes and move away from our addictions. Because isn't that what hope and recovery is all about, Mr. Epstein?"

Mr. Epstein had nothing to say and neither did anyone else in that room. In fact, everyone was shocked to know that I was once an alcoholic, and that I was once, and was at that time, homeless.

After two months at the hotel, Social Services threatened to take my children if I did not have housing for us before school started again. I woke up then and got proactive. I sent Ken home to his brother's house so we would stop arguing with each other, I insisted the kids stay with Gabriel at his house, and I spent the days searching for the right home for us. I found it in Lakeridge, and on July 3, 2009, we moved into our new forever home without furniture. Two weeks later, I sent for Ken after housing gave us the okay to move our furniture in. The fighting between Ken and I and the children resumed.

Our home was a constant battlefield. Ken hated the kids. The kids hated Ken. I hated all the fighting and growing up. The kids hated my inattentiveness and my embracing my agoraphobia. They hated the fighting and continual anger. No one was happy. But outside my home I had to keep putting up a façade of being okay and having it all together. At church I sang solos and taught Sunday school on Wednesday nights and served as an Awana leader on Sundays. At work during the week, I taught WRAP workshops that led people to hope in recovering from mental illness and other medical crises that might come their way. During the week I tirelessly worked to talk people down and out of suicide, and I tried to persuade them to turn away from drugs and alcohol and turn their hearts to Jesus.

One uncommon afternoon while the children were at school, my father came to my house. What made this uncommon is that he never came to my house after Ken and I were married. I invited my father inside, offered him a drink, and sat opposite to him. The first thing he said turned me upside down.

"So, Vicki, explain to me what salvation means."

Here was my father, an avid black Muslim, who prayed five times a day and read the Quran faithfully. He had disowned me for turning away from the faith. This was the same man who made me homeless for the first time in my life because I refused to have sex with him, and yet here he was sitting in my living room, drinking my tea, and asking me about Jesus. I reached for my Bible, and for several hours my father and I went through the scriptures together. And I allowed the scriptures to speak to my father about the cross work of Christ. During that time, God spoke to both of us about why Jesus came to die.

We had made a fatal mistake as humanity. We chose to disobey God when we were given the chance to choose to obey him freely of ourselves. As a result of our wrong choice, sin was introduced into the world. But God loved us so much, he gave us the chance to admit our failure, repent, ask for forgiveness, and turn away from our sin. Being the loving father that he is, he would have forgiven us. Therefore, God went looking for Adam and Eve when they were hiding from God in the garden. He knew where they were; it was no surprise to him. He wanted to give us the chance to redeem ourselves; that is what love does. But instead, out of our own pride, we refused to acknowledge our sin. Instead we blamed everyone and everything else. So God had to let us know the consequences for our bad choices, and we were cast out of the garden and into the world. But God, being the good father that he is, cannot leave his children without hope, so he gave up the one thing that was most precious to him—his son.

Jesus was born to die. Scripture tells us that the wages of sin is death. The price had to be paid, and the only way I could pay for my sins was that I would have to die and eternally burn in hell forever. Our Heavenly Father, being the good father that Daddy is, gave Jesus up as payment for the price of sin. Jesus willingly did all the cross work purposely to the glory of the Father and for the sake of God's lost children. And then Jesus conquered the grave and death by raising himself from the dead on the third day. And now each one of us can come to the Father on our own and ask forgiveness for our sins, humbly recognizing our need for a savior and our inability to save ourselves.

I tried searching out every single scripture passage that I could remember and that I could find about salvation and the cross work of Christ. After three hours of this discussion and my father intensely listening, he got up and told me thank you. then he left. I thought nothing of this afterwards. I tirelessly painted paintings; I entered competitions and hung them in libraries. I tirelessly wrote poetry and entered it in competitions and magazines. I was revved up and doing so many things at the same time, running away from the past and searching for a new today. In all my running and activities, I pushed everyone around me farther away.

One day I got a call from my father's doctor. My father was at the hospital in the middle of surgery. He named me his power of attorney and he needed me. Why would my father make me power of attorney? He had disowned me, so why me? Nevertheless, I got dressed and waddled over to the hospital surgery room. I waited in the hall for my father to come out of surgery. The doctor came out and let me know that their attempt to unclog the arteries in my father's leg and two arteries in his heart were unsuccessful. They were damaged beyond repair. He was 85, and his time was short. They rolled my father upstairs into the ICU to his room. By the time I got up there to see him, he was awake and smiling. My dad was smiling. My dad never smiled. He was never happy. Yet here he was, sitting and smiling and happy. What was he so happy about? The doctors were not able to do what they attempted to do during surgery, which was to unclog his arteries and lengthen his life. So why was he happy? In his room, my pastor and one of the elders from my church were there. When my father saw me coming in, he said "Wonderful, let us get this party started. Isn't this the part when we pray?"

"What do you mean, Dad," I asked?

"Well," he said "I gave my heart to Jesus just like you talked about with me, so isn't this the time we all are supposed to pray so I can ask God into my heart and be saved?"

I did not know what to say. I know God was a miracle-working God, but this was one of those impossible prayers that was happening before my eyes. All of us were silent for a long time. Then Dad said, "Did you guys not hear me? Aren't we supposed to pray?"

"Yes, dad, I am just shocked. You do not know how long I have been praying for you."

"Yes, I do. You have been praying for me since the day you became a Christian and I stopped talking to you. What you did not know was from that day forward, God was working on me, and I was fighting him. But God always wins out. So let's pray now." And that is what we all did.

In October of 2009, a pandemic hit our community: H1N1. People were dropping like flies and dying from this severe flu-like illness. We were not spared. During all of our anger and fighting, all of us (except Gladys) were struck down with H1N1. We ended up in the emergency room on IVs. I was admitted because I was pregnant with Emmanuel. They determined to pump me full of antibiotics, then take Emmanuel early before the H1N1 could get to him and kill him. I was a walking time bomb without knowing it. A week later they took Emmanuel out of my womb. While I was birthing him, my heart stopped. I felt my breath go and my brain was on fire. I reached up and clutched the arm of the nurse that was telling me to push. I breathlessly tried to say, "I cannot breathe." I do not know if she heard me. They took an EpiPen and put it into my chest. Suddenly I could breathe and I pushed for Emmanuel to be born. It was the hardest birth experience I ever had.

I wanted to stay at the hospital for weeks, but on the second day they packed me up to go home. I told the doctor that I felt so weak, and my limbs felt so heavy. It was a weird tired. I did not want to go home. But the doctors decided to send me home anyway. Once home, I never left the couch. For close to two weeks, I laid there on the couch neither eating nor getting up. My limbs felt so heavy and my chest hurt when I tried to exert energy or raise my voice over a whisper. My brain stayed foggy and tired as if I had just fought a civil war. Ken tried to be kind, and the kids were very mindful. The house stayed quiet and pensive as if everyone were waiting for something bad to happen. Finally, Ken could not take it anymore. He called the emergency room and scooped me up. Bye then, my skin was turning a yellowy grey and my eyes were swimming in yellow at half-mast. Once at the emergency room, he forced me out of the car. I stood up feeling like cement was in my arms and legs pulling me down to the ground. I watched the nurses running up to me with a wheelchair. Sound around me was like a tunnel, so far away and low. Then everything went black. I came to float above my body as I was being wheeled into the ICU. I watched them put the tube down my throat and hook me to several machines. I kept asking what was going on, but no one heard me. I was dead and my spirit was released above me. They were trying to save my life; a life I had thrown away. When I came to again, I was laying in the bed and I was very scared. My room door opened, and a small Asian doctor walked in. He was surrounded by light. He took my hand and smiled, assuring me I would be okay. "Don't be afraid; you are not going to die. You will be fine. Everything will be fine." His soft voice and gentle touch were reassuring. I calmed down and accepted my situation. I went back to sleep.

CHAPTER ELEVEN

Heartless

Once I came home, Ken decided to go back home with his twin brother, Tim, and live in Fredericksburg. "I didn't sign up for this," he said referring to the possibility of caring for six children on his own and a few years without sex. I did not blame him, and if I were in his shoes, I probably would have asked the same thing, being overwhelmed by the circumstances. I had not been kind to him, so there really was not anything to hold him there. So, I did not fight him; rather I let him go. I figured after three months or so he would be back, assuming I was doing much better, so I said go.

I was too weak to climb downstairs the first three months. Emmanuel was a few months old and Anna was two years old. My daughter Gladys requested to be homeschooled because of social troubles at school. And seeing how I was struggling to take care of the little ones as well as them without falling asleep or needing to take long breaks sitting down because of fatigue, she asked if she could help at home. She later regretted this offer, and so did I. She missed so much of her teen years. It was not fair to her. The whole situation made her grow up too fast, and the older she got, the angrier she became. She holds on to that anger to this day.

For a short while, Gabriel from church came and helped at my house, too. Just when I needed a Superman, there he was. When he was done working as an auto mechanic, he would drive over to my home and help the children with their chores and their homework. I would sit on the steps and watch as she helped, and the children would be smiling and talking, content that someone else cared. This was the reason Gabriel had always been my guardian angel and my hero. From the time I was 16 and came to that youth group meeting that he was helping to lead, Gabriel had been my hero. He could do no wrong. This charismatic and charming man with the bright smile and over-the-top personality was the one that watched over me and brought me peace. I was so enamored with Gabriel that I did not realize how high of a pedestal I put him on—sometimes higher than God. I had never met a person who I truly believed loved me and cherished me with his whole heart to the point that he was willing to sacrifice his time to come to my house and help me and my children. We had no romantic or blood connections, only friendship. This strong bond demonstrated to me the love that God has for his children. It reminded me that no matter what, God would never abandon us but would always be there for us because of his love. This is what I saw in Gabriel, and this is what made me so stubbornly loyal to him no matter what.

When I was stronger and able to go down the steps, I tried going grocery shopping, but I could not remember why I was there or how to manage shopping. Another time I tried going back to work, but I was confused and argumentative, so they let me go. The perpetual happy face I once owned was gone. In its place was confusion and frustration. No one knew what to do with me. I was always ready for battle verbally, and did not stop till I thought I won. If I got wound up, I did not know how to stop; my voice would get louder and louder and high-pitched. I would go on and on sometimes for hours, often repeating myself without knowing it. This drove my kids nuts. Then I would walk away forgetting what the argument was over to begin with. It was frustrating. It was like I did not understand them, and it made my kids feel like I was unjust. My changeable emotions left me breathless and everyone else uncomfortable.

Three months after I prayed with my father to receive Christ, he died in his sleep. But before he did, my father finally said, "I love you." The night he died was our last night talking. I can still remember his voice. He said he did not feel all that great. He felt like he had a cold that he could not shake, and he wanted me to pray for him. I did and I told him not to worry; we had been down this road before. A year after my father's passing, the confusion, perpetual depression, and loss of friends and family became overwhelming. Many of my friends fell away because of my change in personality. And my family (that is, my brothers) distance themselves from me, because my father never changed his will. It still indicated that I was disowned, even though my dad did make some provisions.

The week that I called my case manager and asked for help, my oldest daughter and her aunt were over visiting. I was trying very hard to reconcile with Rachel. Rachel left home at 16 when the court sent her brother Joseph away. Even though we all had come back together again as a family, Rachel never forgave me for not being there to protect her from Howard. No amount of apologizing could heal that wound. So for years after, I tried to relieve things. I would send letters to her father's house, at first almost every day, and then finally monthly until he moved. Once he moved, I had no address to send them to.

When computers became the thing, I found her online on this new thing called Facebook, and I attempted to reconcile our relationship. After the death of my father when she came to the funeral, I tried once again face-to-face. But Rachel refused to look at me in the face or even talk to me. Instead she talked at me or talked to someone else, asking them to relay her message to me as if I were not in the room. This hurt very deeply. If I could take the events of that time away, God knows I would. But how was it possible in 2001 and 2002 to know whether someone was a criminal or not? There was no public database to Google as there is today. The laws were different, and Howard's family was not talking; neither were his friends. I had no idea really who he was, except how he presented himself to me and to our church family. He was the coach of the girls' softball team, and he was a foster care parent in three counties. He also was the president of the housing association in our area. By every standard, everything checked out. He was about 20 years older than me, but I was fine with that because I just wanted someone to love me without wanting to have sex with me. So it seemed to work. He was lonely and wanted companionship. I was working myself to death, and my injuries were not healing as quickly as they could have if I were not working and taxing myself. I wanted to be home and raise my children like I was doing before. This would have been a good situation for God to have glued a sign to his forehead saying to me, "Criminal! Run away!" But no such thing existed, and I was caught unawares, as well as seven other families in our community whose children were raped or molested by this monster. Rachel had the courage to speak up and tell someone, saving all those children besides her siblings. Once charges were brought against him, the other seven spoke up. But by then, the damage was done. At the time of my father's funeral, we had not spoken face-to-face in years.

I felt like something else happened besides the heart attack. I just was not myself. I knew I was not crazy, but all the uncontrollable crying, the arguing, the lack of memory, and the difficulty focusing on just one thing was overwhelming. So, I went to my counselor's office in tears and said "Please help me. I do not know what is wrong with me."

My counselor walked out saying he would be right back with some help. I assumed he was going to take me somewhere to be tested. Instead of that, in walked three beefy officers. They handcuffed me, walked me down the hall and through the packed lunchroom outside, then frisked me up against the police cars. I was in shock. I was driven like a criminal to the psychiatric ward and held against my will for three months on high doses of psychotropic drugs. No one told my family of my whereabouts for three days until I was finally allowed to call. To my older kids it looked like I walked out and abandoned them. They were left to fend for themselves. I begged others in my church and family to please care for my kids, but my request was ignored. They spent three months raising themselves. The one time they came to see me, they looked stunned. Did their mother go crazy? Were they about to lose their mom, too?

CHAPTER TWELVE

A Reckoning

When I came home high on the psychotropic medications, I walked into a flooded house covered in mildew. At some point the kids went to stay with someone in the church. The house was locked up and shut. It was the year northern Virginia survived its first earthquake. Right on its coat tails, we had monsoon rains that were unbelievable. The entire cul-de-sac flooded, but my home was the only one not cleaned out.

The smell of stale water was putrid. We could not stay there. We ended up being split up again for another two months while I tried to convince my property owner to fix the damage. I watched as 80 percent of my belongings and furniture was thrown into the back of a truck and thrown away. All these events left the children and I stunned. Once again Gabriel was there to save the day, offering his truck, the vehicle used to take my damaged goods away. I was so brokenhearted. We were staying in a hotel because we had no other place to go, and on the eighth day Gabriel came and said he found a house just right for me and my family. He promised that if everything worked out right after a year of renting from the landlord, he would buy the house and become my landlord. I would never have to worry about being homeless ever again. Gabriel was living up to my notion of him as my hero, and his pedestal grew higher as we moved into the house on Kern Dale.

My friend Gabriel became like a guardian to me after my test results came back showing a brain injury due to hypoxia from the heart attack. They were not sure how mild or severe, but what they did know was that it was interrupting my life and making survival extremely difficult. So I agreed. Who better than my best friend and my hero? He put us up in a hotel so we all could be together again, out of his own pocket. Then he found the perfect house for us to rent. He said my property owner was unwilling to clean up and fix the damage. The house became condemned by the health department. I thought I found a good thing in Gabriel becoming my "guardian." I took the entire basement for my bedroom, and the kids occupied upstairs. We were finally home.

As a family we were very broken and hurting in our own individual ways. We were all missing Rachel and Joseph, whom we had difficulty seeing and hearing from. We learned Rachel was getting married, and we all wanted to go, but then we got a knock on our door. It was one of sixteen visits from Child Protective Services. This first visit they felt something was off. The accusations that had been leveled at me did not hold up. The investigator warned me that I could not associate with certain family members for a year while they investigated. They could not give me specific names of those being investigated by them, but one of those persons was my daughter, Rachel. I was devastated as were the other kids. They advocated hard for going to the wedding anyway, despite the authorities' warning and the warning I later received from family not to go. My family at this point assumed I was crazy, and they had a running joke that I was schizophrenic and dangerous. Of course, I was not, but it was a family joke and I was not laughing.

This revelation brought morale down even more in my home. Why did these things keep happening to us? The kids stayed angry with me for the longest time. Gladys did not want to talk to me, and she would lock herself in her room refusing to see me. Suzan spent a lot of time with her school friends and at color guard practice. She tried very hard to avoid home altogether. Samuel did similar to Suzan. He spent time after school practicing soccer or hanging out with school friends. Anna and Emmanuel were toddlers and missed the activities of their older siblings. They did not understand what was happening.

Less than a year had gone by in our new home before the property owner insisted we buy the property for three times more than what it was worth, according to Gabriel. Gabriel said he could not do that so he refused, and she gave us 72 hours to get out or she would evict us. This was brought to my attention after a wonderful day at Great Falls. Housing called me in with Gabriel and informed me if I stayed and fought, the rent would be my responsibility. I would lose the voucher. Gabriel and some others came, packed up my house, and moved us into storage.

One of those people who helped pack me up was Gary. Gary and I had briefly dated when I first moved into the area. We broke up because it was hard being a mixed couple, and he wanted a lot that I could not give him. Gabriel reached out to him for help, and he came. In three days, my house sat in storage.

I dropped my marble dining table on my foot and broke it in two places. Here I was homeless in a hotel with a boot on my foot, crutches, and no food with my children in Stafford away from me once more. I wanted to stay with them, but housing said no. If I did, they would move my case to Stafford. I did not want to move to Stafford.

For nine weeks I was forced to be homeless. The first two weeks, I lived in a hotel on Route 1. I was not driving, had no car, and had a broken foot, so I could not get any food. I stayed there with nothing but me and a few things in my bag. The money ran out and I stood on the edge of Route 1 unsure what to do. I went back to the hotel and called Gabriel. He angrily came and paid for two more days at the hotel. I did not understand why he was so angry with me. It was not my fault that I lost my home. I was not ready to move again, and I had no money. All my money had been spent when I tried to be a first-time homebuyer and when I came home from the hospital, and we had to stay at a hotel because the house flooded.

During that time Gary suddenly showed up and took me to his house. He offered for me to stay there. I was grateful, but his roommate attacked me a few times. His roommate saw my being there as an opportunity to get with me. I was not interested, and he was not trying to be a gentleman. For some reason Gary never tried to protect me, so I left and I spent four weeks homeless on the street sleeping in the library, emergency room, and IHOP. I even broke into my home church to sleep in the baptismal fount. I finally could not take it. I spent the last two weeks locking myself up in Gary's room.

This four-year journey I just described was incredible, and it had lasting effects on myself and my children. The children came out of it feeling abandoned by their mom and without family. I came out of it broken and untrusting. Homelessness does something to your brain. It makes you unhinged in your thinking and emotions. I began to doubt everything, trust nothing, and fear the worst.

During this four-year ride, I began to drink again. I was proud of my ten-year sobriety, but the overwhelming emotions and pain I endured losing so much and being separated from my children was too much. Because my room was in the basement, it had been easy to lock the door and disappear into a drunken stupor till I went to sleep. I hid my bad habit from my children once more, choosing to drink only at night, alone in my room, when my witching hour would come on. While I was homeless, it was harder to get alcohol, so I drank mouthwash and Nyquil. Moving into the new apartment, I continued to drink excessive amounts of Listerine mouthwash and anything else. I could not handle the strong emotions that came with knowing how my older kids were feeling and how angry they were, as well as the fear of losing my home again or being locked up once more. The drinking started having negative effects on my health. I got a serious scare when I started hemorrhaging anally. I was in a spiritual crisis. I had been oblivious to what this crisis was until I started hemorrhaging.

All this time since I moved back after Howard, I had been wandering in the desert without God. I went to church, I served in church, and I even talked to people about Jesus. But all that time, I did not trust him. In fact, I did not look to him for my help or comfort. Rather I was looking to Gabriel and Gary and my church to be my protectors and to care for me. God for me had taken a back seat. I believed very strongly that I was cursed and that there was nothing that I could do about it but endure. I had decided all those years ago that God loved me as his creation, but he did not love me personally. I was too much of a failure, and just like my dad, God could not accept me. He only showed me grace or mercy because of my children. They did not ask to be born, and all that had happened up to this point was not their fault. I should have been a better mother and protected them, but I did not. So I believed that God was punishing me, and that's why all the bad things kept happening. Gabriel and Gary were the only good things in my life besides my children.

When I started hemorrhaging, it was as if God stepped back into my life. The truth is that he never left. He had always been there. It was me who had walked away from him, and when I was laying in the hospital being treated and getting blood transfusions, it was me who turned back to God. I stopped drinking for good. Even though I stopped, the health issues continued. I began to have a series of strokes. With every stroke, I began to talk to God once again. I also began to acknowledge the existence of my dark friend who was ever watching us. I began to pray that God would keep him from hurting us.

In December 2015, my son Samuel found me passed out across my bed hemorrhaging once more. He called 911. I spent four weeks in the hospital and received two blood transfusions. I had to have surgery and have an ostomy made. At some point after surgery, in recovery, I stroked out again. Our world was about to turn upside down once more.

CHAPTER THIRTEEN

Transformation

It was Christmas in December 2015, and I was laid up in the hospital receiving two blood transfusions. How did I get here? Oh, I know how I got here. Everything we do in the dark always comes out into the light. I guess it was my turn. Even though I had gone into sobriety June of 2003, I lost my sobriety after coming home from the Northern Virginia Psychiatric Ward. Everything had changed when I came home. The medication they put me on made me drowsy and inattentive. I could not feel or react to things properly. I had nightmares of my life nightly, and during the day I saw phantoms of the ghost past and the fears of what was to come. Suicide was like a cloth blanket that I clung to; my escape route if I could not bear the difficulties of life anymore. I had a complete plan laid out, and I found comfort in it by obsessing on it. Leaving my children was the only thing that made me hesitate. But it did not hold me back from dwelling on it.

I had made a new friend, Alexis, at church. It was the first time in years that I had a girlfriend. She felt hopeless about her life too. She was bipolar and was struggling with her mental health and multiple sclerosis. She self-medicated with marijuana and cocaine. But her favorite poison was alcohol, vodka. When we got together, she would offer it to me constantly and I would turn her down. I did not want to lose my kids. But I had no trouble going with her to pick some up. My on-and-off boyfriend, Gary, made homemade moonshine from apples. I warmed her up to his product, and she started to buy it. It was 20 proof; strong. Many times when Gary and I got together, Gary would be drunk, or at least tipsy. Temptation surrounded me. The alcohol seemed to help Alexis forget her problems and be funny. She was forever having all of us in stitches; she was the female version of Jim Carrey. No one was as funny and quick with the quips as she was. If she only had the confidence in herself, she would have been an award-winning stand-up comedian. Gary loosened up when he was tipsy or drunk. The sweet romantic side of him would come out, and he would talk and treat me so tenderly. I never knew another man who could be so tender and intimate with me as Gary. He truly seemed to love me deeply, I thought. I wanted the same sweet release I thought I saw in both. I longed for my pain to be numbed up like them, to relax and unwind and not be under the control of the painful past or the anxiety-filled present. So, I fell, and I fell hard.

When I could buy alcohol, I hid it in my room under my bed, and I would lock myself in my room at night and chug drink while watching movies. Other times I would drink on my swing outside at night while looking up at the moon. I would go through two to three whole bottles of vodka or vodka and wine, straight. Sometimes before I fell asleep, I would hug the toilet while I vomited into it. Other times, it would not hit me till the morning. But the buzz in my head and the warmness in my chest and stomach was an incredible hug of comfort for the moment. In the morning, the raging headache and dull depression would set in once again. I would take my medication and numb up all over. When I could not afford the alcohol, I had learned during the time I was homeless to buy bottles of Listerine mouthwash. It took a lot more to get drunk, but it was achievable.

Then I learned an extremely sickening trick. There was a faster way to get drunk without spending as much money, and it covered any smell of alcohol. I learned to put alcohol in an enema and feed it to myself that way. In this way, my nightly drinking turned to morning, afternoon, and nightly drinking through the enema. The feeling of drunkenness was immediate and strong. I learned to use just so much. It seemed to give me the confidence I longed for to stand before others and teach workshops, to stand up in church and sing solos weekly, to stand up and actively teach Sunday school. It enabled me to speak my mind when I felt attacked by others, and do so with confidence. I felt empowered, but I also felt I found the aphrodisiac I needed to forget my pain and move forward.

Unfortunately, because of what I started doing, I did not realize how much I was harming my body at an accelerated rate. At first, I would see spots of blood from my anus. The doctor said I had bad hemorrhoids from Crohn's disease, and every so often I had to go into his office and get them catharized so they would stop bleeding. Eventually that did not work anymore, and spotting turned to hemorrhaging large amounts of blood in the toilet. Now my doctor was concerned. The "hemorrhoids" were no longer just on the outside, they were now internal. My doctor was perplexed. He did not know how it was happening. So he blamed it on my diet.

During this time, in 2013 and then again in 2014, I suffered two strokes, one major and the other minor. They both seemed to come out of left field, and it left my heart doctor perplexed too. My heart had become weak again. In September of 2015, I went to war with my boss on the Fairfax WRAP team because of her desire to use me as a way of convincing one of our constituents for more grant money, and I lost my job for a time as a result of my resistance to play along. After that happened, I began to hemorrhage uncontrollably. The blood was purply red in the toilet. I was rushed to the emergency room. My doctor, assuming my Crohn's disease had become unmanageable, began talking about me having surgery for an ostomy. An ostomy; only old people got that. I watched videos on it and read up on it. I had to face the fact that I did this to me. How could I face any of the people I had helped or my children with the knowledge that I did this to feed my addiction? Once I came home from the hospital, I threw away my enema kit and swore off the alcohol. I assumed God would forgive me. It was our secret and a secret it would stay, I believed.

But on December 20, 2015, I began to hemorrhage once again uncontrollably, and I passed out on my bed coming out of the bathroom. I woke up in the emergency room on a bed. I got up and tried to walk to the bathroom.

I could hear the nurse behind me asking me what I was doing as I felt my knees buckle from under me. I laid my face down on the cold linoleum floor still on my knees and went to sleep. Blood pooled all over the floor around me, but I had no idea. I had passed out. Now here I was, laid up in my hospital bed on Christmas day alone. The same time I swore off the alcohol and lost my job, I broke up with Gary and I ended my friendship with Alexis. I was alone, except for my kids and Gabriel, my guardian angel. I felt I did not need anyone else. But laying in that hospital bed on Christmas Day, it came crashing down on me how wrong I was. I was so hung up on running away from the pain of the past, and so caught up in all the anxiety of the present and how I could self-medicate, I did not see what was happening in life around me. Since 2011, my older kids had made up their determined minds as a collective to be their own family. They felt I had abandoned them. Even when I was there, I was not there, and they felt that pain every day. I gave no notice to others who had moved into my home and took over being mommy and daddy to my kids. I was blind to what was hurting them because I was running away from all that was hurting me.

By the time 2015 rolled around, I had lost all of my kids but one, Samuel, but I was blind to that fact. Laying in that hospital bed brought it all home. My kids were nowhere. None of them came to sit beside me, to keep me company, or to try to assist in this critical time in my life. They were completely absent. They had abandoned me. I looked for Gabriel and he was supposedly out of town in West Virginia with his grandmother. No one from the church I belonged to was there, either, nor did anyone from the church offer to visit or find out what was going on. I was completely alone. A few times I called Gary's number, then hung up. I could not go back to the past. The despair I faced was overwhelming. The doctor told me I would need surgery. My colon was dead, and I had become septic. They had to remove my colon and parts of my large intestine. They would create an ostomy for me and that would relieve the Crohn's disease. If I chose to do nothing, I would have less than six months to live. With surgery, my heart was weak; this decreased my chances of survival having surgery. I had to choose. I chose surgery with the knowledge that I may not make it, and that if I did, I might possibly stroke out, or worse, have a heart attack and die. Morbidly, the knowledge of possibly dying gave me misplaced comfort.

After a month in the hospital, I was told I had to leave for two weeks then come back for surgery. The reason for this was my insurance had run out. However, because of my condition, I had to stay with someone. I called around to almost everyone I could think of, but no one would come and get me. All my adult children refused to help in any way. Some of them were in college and could not. My brothers, Cliff and Brian, completely refused to help or to take me. My brother Nathan rushed to my side when the hospital called him, but he lived in a group apartment with a bunch of other guys. It just was not ideal. Nathan stayed with me the rest of the time. Joseph also came to my side when called by the hospital. He and his wife were staying with their landlord. It seemed hopeful until they both began to fight in my room. Security had to come and escort them out. Opportunity lost. I had no choice:

I called Alexis. Alexis left her job and came and picked me up. I stayed with her in her basement for two weeks. She was the best nurse and friend during that time. I regretted ending our friendship. I do not remember if she drank or did drugs during that time. I did have the best conversations and girl time.

When I went into surgery on February 2, 2016, I had put my house in order, wrote my goodbye notes, said goodbye on Facebook in a cryptic way, and prepared to meet my Father God in heaven. In a perverse way, I was happy that I was about to die. The pain would be over, the rejection and loss would be gone, erased from my mind. Never again would I feel that prick of pain in my heart as I dwelled on Howard hurting my Rachel, or my father and Jacob hurting and abusing my Joseph, or the deep sadness I saw in the eyes of my Gladys, the struggle my Suzan daily fought fighting back her own tears, the memories of being slapped down by Jacob or raised up in the air by my throat, feet off the ground, unable to breathe because I displeased him in some way or other. Never again would I hold onto the memory of Howard's fist coming to my face, or the kids laughing at me and throwing pennies and spit wads at my hair. Never again, the nightmare of my dad coming to my room in the middle of the night, the clanging of his keys, and the slamming of the front door. All these sorrows would be over; gone. As the anesthesia put me out and I began to count backwards, I relished the hope of seeing God. I wanted so much to lay my head on the bosom of Jesus forever. I wanted that eternal peace everyone talked about in church. An end to life and the beginning of eternal bliss. But, in that empty darkness and swirling colors of nothingness, I sat across from him. The dark shadow that haunted my life since I was a baby. He sat in his chair, legs crossed looking at me with great intensity, waiting for me to wake up to the reality that the heaven I hoped to enter had not come to fruition. I sat on a hard, wooden kitchen chair.

"Why are you in this empty, open-aired room above and below life, looking at me, your enemy? Why? What are you looking for?" he asked me without moving his lips.

"I am looking for love. I am looking for heaven, I want to go to heaven!" I yelled at him without moving my own lips.

"This is not heaven," he replied. "It is not hell either, Vicky. You did it all wrong."

"No, no, there is some mistake," I said. "I did not live wrong. I did the best I possibly could. What do you mean wrong? The sacrifices I made for so many people. I put up with all the pain and hurt. I made the right choices. I did life right. It was life that did me wrong."

"Really?" he said.

I felt like all of heaven was listening to me.

"This is not fair," I said. "I could have let my parents adopt my kids, but I did not. They lost their dad to that bimbo; they did not need to lose me too. So I said no. That was the right thing to do. I raised them as best I could. I made that deal with Howard because I could not work three jobs anymore. I was being responsible. I sought out a father for them. Children need a family. I did the right thing. He was the unfaithful one, not me. And I worked hard to prove to the courts that I could

take care of my kids. I took all their classes; I got a job; I joined a church; I went to the vocational center; I got my act together. I spent $6,000 on a lawyer and bought my children back. How many parents can say they did that? That is how precious they were to me."

The devil looked at me unconvinced. By now, I was on my feet in defense of myself.

"I took the medication they gave me religiously; I taught others to do the same and live in recovery. I became a spokesman for recovery. I am in a book, a movie, pamphlets. I did more than most. I spoke to senators and representatives, all for the cause of mental health and recovery. I was a mentor and an example of the recovery movement. And look at what I was doing in the church. I sang a solo once a week. I worked hard at making my musical craft perfect. I was the best, all for the glory of God."

"I am sure you were Vicky," he replied.

"I was. And I even went back to school. After 17 years, I finally got my bachelor's degree when no one thought I could. I am a success. People look up to me. I did well."

"Well," he mocked, "then why are you drinking? Why are you chasing an addiction you yourself speak strongly against? Why did you not take the time to spend time with your children? You yelled at them and pushed them. But did you ever think to sit down and talk to them? Did they say they wanted another father? So now God builds marriages on business agreements? Did you pray about whether God wanted you to be married? I thought I remembered a young

18-year-old fervently praying to God one moonlit night in Newberry, South Carolina, how, if it was God's will for you to be single, you would dedicate your life in service to Him as His missionary. Am I correct, or was that someone else? Maybe it was a childish prayer because you did not take the time to wait for the answer God had for you. Instead you assumed that your parents saying yes to Jacob's proposal meant God wanted you to get married. But if you had listened to him in that Sunday school room on your wedding day, if you had held back your tears and listened, He would have told you, 'Vicky, run. This is not what I want for you. Run Vicky, run.' No, instead, you listened to me. You listened to your feelings and let them speak for you. My voice spoke to you, Vicky. God's voice was silent because you listened to me more than you listened to Him. I told you what you wanted to hear."

"No," I cried out. "I did not want to get married, I wanted to get away from my father."

"Then why did you get married?"

I could not answer him.

"You did not love him to lay down with him. So why? Husbands and wives make love; you could not, so why? And why did you volunteer to raise those kids as a single parent? You were still recovering from the car accident I tried so desperately to take your life with. Why would you volunteer to move from your parents' house and raise those kids on your own? You could not. You were socially of the mind of a third-grader. Your brain was still scrambled. Your parents were trying to

help because they recognized you were childlike at that point. Why did you not listen?"

"I did not want them to be without me," I said.

"They would not have been," he said. "So much hardship would have been avoided if you did not listen to your feelings, if you had trusted those around you, if you were not listening to your pride."

"The sinking despair in life was seeping back into my heart in this nothingness place," I said.

"And an example?" he sneered, "You wanted to kill yourself. You slowly worked to kill yourself with alcohol and mouthwash through what? An enema?

"Who does that?" he snickered. "I never thought you would listen to that suggestion from me. You were so proud of your sobriety. How stupid could you be? You are a drunkard, an addict. You are the worst of the worst, not an example to be emulated. You do not think your kids did not know? While you were enjoying your fetish, your girls were crying, some talked about running away, some were wishing they had their parents back, some even considered suicide. Your kids were tempted by sex, drugs, bitterness, and hate because of their own pain. Where were you? Locked in your room and feeling sorry for yourself. An example, hypocrite. Pitiful hypocrite. Yeah, you sang God's praises in the church and you meant every word, but that voice was your pride. You worshipped that voice more than you worshipped God."

"No! You are wrong," I said.

"No, I am not," he replied. "If your voice were taken away, how many times did you say you would

die? If you could not sing before others His praises, how many times did you consider dying over not singing before others on Sunday morning?"

I was silent; I knew the answer before he said it.

"You crave everyone's love. You found love in everyone when you stood up there and sang. But you are supposed to be leading everyone into worship, right? Not seeking everyone's love through singing. Hypocrite! You made your voice your God."

"No, stop! No more!"

"Oh, I got more," he continued. "That is my job, the accuser. All your life I followed you, gathering all the reasons I needed to accuse you before Him, and you gladly supplied me. You have been so deaf to His voice and blind to His love; it was easy.

"You'd rather prepare for death and hope for it to come quickly than fulfill your promise and serve Him in your calling," he laughed.

"Am I going to hell?" I asked.

He just kept laughing at me.

"Am I going to hell? I do not want to go to hell. I am saved, I am saved."

"What good did that do you?" he mocked me. "Look at you; He cannot use you. Addict, drunkard, arrogant, selfish, you might as well give up and come with me."

"But I am saved," I said. "How could I fail so miserably, and yet I am saved?"

"Saved, yes," he laughed, "but you never let Him sanctify you. You never allowed the Holy Spirit to sanctify you in your life."

"But I served in the church, in the community. I did good things; how could it be?"

"For the Holy Spirit to sanctify you, you must be willing to go through affliction, trouble, hurt, and pain. Without these things, you can never learn how to truly love like Him. You must feel pain, go through pain, to know how to truly love others. You must be willing to feel lovelessness to love with Agape love. I get you fools every time. I told Him, none of you want to know pain. You all want to know power and control; none of you want to be helpless. That was Eve's problem, that is what caused her to fall. She wanted to be like God on her own terms. You were no different. You thought you could sanctify yourself the way you thought it should be done. And through that you hurt yourself and so many others. Don't you know you cannot sanctify yourself? But you were not listening to anything but your own tears. You were not running from me. You were running from Him."

He laughed. I fell to my knees in acknowledgement of my failure. I failed Him, I failed my children, I failed all those that looked up to me, and I failed myself. He was right; I deserved hell, not heaven. I had been a fool. All this time embracing my painful memories, I ignored the answer to all of it: Jesus. And now, I thought, I was at the end of my life, and it was too late to make up for my mistakes. I left an inheritance of hurt instead of an inheritance of love. I began weeping; not for feeling sorry for myself. For the first time, I was weeping for the lost opportunity to serve God in my promise and bring the love of Christ to those that did not have it. I cried over my hypocrisy and all those I had hurt by being fake and unfaithful, whether they knew it or not.

I awaited the cold emptiness of death to steal me away into the fires of hell. But instead, the warmth of God's love enveloped me in a way no amount of alcohol could. That is when I noticed, he was not laughing at me anymore. God was calling my name, softly, gently.

"Vicky, daughter, do you hear me?"

"Yes, yes, Father, I hear you."

"Go home and do my will," He said.

"What if I fail?" I asked. "I do not want to live. I failed you so badly."

"Go home, I am with you," He replied. "I never left you. You left me, but I stayed. Go home, I am with you. I will show you what to say and what to do. Do not be afraid."

"But the Holy Spirit, I never let Him sanctify me," I said. "How can I do anything right, God? I made a mess of my life."

God giggled.

"I sanctify you every day, Vicky," He said. "I work in your life, My will to My glory, and now you will know that every day. For now on, you will know I am near; you will listen to me and you will see Me. Through every affliction, through every problem and pain, I will be there. You will know it, you will hear Me, and you will follow Me, because now you know I love you. You will love Me, and you will love others for Me to My glory."

"Help me God, help me!" I begged Him.

I woke up in that hospital bed saying "Help me!"

A major stroke sometime after the surgery left my left foot curled in, my left arm limp like a noodle, my face drooped, and my words scrambled. There were holes in my memory that made it hard for me to find words and to remember simple things. It was frustrating. But before I could start any physical therapy, I had an infection in my ostomy that I had to battle, and it left me soaked in sweat from daily battling fever. My body was weak and impotent. I could do nothing but lay in my hospital bed listening to my roommate snoring.

"Are you kidding me God?" I said. "I came back for this?"

"No, you came back for Me," I heard Him say.

"God, did you just talk to me?"

"I always was; you just were not listening." He said.

Before when I heard that voice, I wanted to brush it away as me talking to myself, but I could not deny it. God was talking to me, and my roommates snoring was unbearably loud.

"Okay God, you proved to me you have a sense of humor; could you please quiet my roommate?"

"No, I cannot," He said quite clearly. "Remember, I am with you through affliction, and I will provide you a way out, but you must be willing to take it. That is sanctification."

"Snoring? Snoring is sanctification, God, really?"

"Vicky, is her snoring causing you pain? Are you feeling afflicted?"

"Yes, dear Lord, yes," I replied.

"Then You are being tested. Sanctification. What are you going to do about it?"

I thought about that question. Physically, I could do nothing. Even if I tried to talk, at that time, no one might understand me well enough. So, there I laid, afflicted by fever; pain from the infection; a pain in my ears from the snoring. I simply cried till I went to sleep.

During that week He introduced me to a new affliction that drowned out my roommate's continual snoring when she was asleep. Across the hallway was someone in excruciating pain. Every night and throughout the day she cried so pitifully as if in the deepest pain. Other patients would yell for her to shut up. The nurses would come into my room complaining about her never-ending crying. The nights were impossible to get any amount of sleep. The silence was peppered with her whimpering, her weeping, and at times her bawling. As my fever broke, and my strength slowly came back to me, I vowed to find a way to stop her from crying.

***"Why are you concerned about her crying?"* God asked.**

"Lord, no one can sleep."

"What are you going to do about it, Vicky?"

The night came when I stole my roommate's wheelchair, and after struggling to get my broken body into it, I wheeled myself over to her room. I wheeled right into her room, and she sat up and looked at me. It was then that I realized I had boldly gone where I was not supposed to be. It was against the rules for us to go into someone else's room. And she did not know me either; what was I doing?

"Ruth!" she said excitedly. "You came, you came to visit me! Tell me a story."

She begged like a child. I was about to say "I am not Ruth," but something kept my mouth shut.

Instead I said, "What story do you want to hear?"

I told her a story about when we were little. I pretended to be her sister, Ruth, and her face lit up like the sun. When my story was done, she asked me to sing her to sleep, because she was tired and could not sleep. I sang *Over the Rainbow*. It was all I could remember at the time. My voice came out so clear and accurate, like a hummingbird. Her smile was euphoric like a child's on Christmas Day. She closed her eyes to sleep with that smile sealed on it.

I turned to roll out of her room only to be confronted by an audience of surprised nurses. I thought I was in trouble. Instead, they showered me with thank yous.

Things changed after that. Nightly I paid my "sister" a visit and sang to her a song after we had a lively conversation about when we were young. During the day, I visited others and helped to "calm" others down or reassure them that the nice nurse just wanted to feed them or change them. Between the visits and the therapy to get my motor skills and speech back, I forgot my old woes. All that mattered was what was in store for me that day and when I would finally go home. I was finding purpose. Maybe this sanctifying would not be as hard as I thought. Maybe there was no need for me to be running away from my pain. If I had just given it a chance and let myself feel the hurt and pain, maybe things would have been easier and less painful. I left the nursing home after three months feeling like I could do this living thing again, more successfully than I believed myself capable of. But then, does God not have a sense of humor?

CHAPTER FOURTEEN

Victorious One
Chosen of God

When I walked through the front door of my apartment, Samuel was completely overwhelmed and unable to fathom the idea of his mother limping behind a walker. Where did she go? I did not blame him. I was very pensive about coming home as I was. Adult protective services came and visited me at the rehab center and suggested I go live in a retirement community or a nursing home. I seriously considered it. I could not see how I would take care of Emmanuel and Anna in my weakened crippled state. The others were basically grown adults and could manage without me, but the two younger ones? I even went so far as to ask Gabriel to take them and raise them for me. He turned me down, stating he had his mechanical career to think about. I concluded that raising the children myself seemed to be what God wanted me to do, although I still could see no way I could continue to be their parent.

After six weeks of still being on medical leave from my job as a life coach, the company I worked for let me go. I had no extra income to compensate for my little disability check. The new normal was not only my physical change, but also our financial change. It all was part of bringing Samuel down. Instead of being at work helping others to live their lives again despite their disabilities, and teaching them to let go of their addictions and to come out of homelessness, instead of being the care provider to so many people, I was now the one in need of care. Because of the stroke I had suffered after surgery, I was weak on my left side. Everything was affected, and my foot was curled in and slanted. Falling became a regular expectation. At the rehab center, the nurses would come and pick me up and get me back on my feet. But at home, I could be stuck on the floor for hours with no way to get up. The young ones were too young to help me, and Samuel did all he could to avoid being home that first week that I was back.

I cried a lot for no reason, I slept more than I should, I yelled constantly (as my hearing was also affected), I cussed, and I said the first thing I might be thinking. I offended a lot of people that first week. Even at church, you could hear me yelling, or a cuss word would accidently fall out my mouth. It was very shocking. Before the strokes, I never cussed. Now here I was cussing like a sailor, even in front of my children. The lack of control over my emotions and my words became troubling to Samuel, and he decided to run away.

At first, I assumed he was with one of his friends, but after 24 hours, I started to panic. I put an alert out on social media. Thirty minutes later he was home but not happy about it. All the pent-up anger he had over the years came bursting out.

Samuel had always been my angel, the one who let nothing really bother him. As a little one, he was always laughing and smiling. He was an easy kid. While I homeschooled him, and later while he was in public school, he was quiet and reserved; an introvert. But I removed him from his schooling and placed him in private school after the kids in his school regularly bullied him without mercy. Even some of the educational staff joined in, sending him home one day in a pink shirt and shorts because he was pushed by other kids into the creek by the school, getting his original clothes soaked. The embarrassment of being forced to walk around in girls' clothing was too much.

Once in his private school, Samuel blossomed and became an extrovert. It was wonderful watching my good boy turn into the charismatic man in love with Jesus. By the time he was a teenager, he would go around to different other schools and preach about the goodness of the Lord in his life. I was so proud of him. He was doing very well for himself, I believed.

When he let out all his anger that day, I was caught by surprise. I did not realize how angry he was over what happened with Howard, over being poor and having nothing, over being raised by a single, disabled mother and the impact of my disability had on him, and how angry he was now as he was tired of all my absences and inabilities. While at the rehab center, my therapist worked on me to have a sense of humor. Personality wise, I smiled a lot to be respectful and polite, but I naturally was very serious and prone to seeing things negatively.

She suggested that I watch comedians and films that were comedies. Read books with jokes and learn to tell my own. I learned a lot of innocent and dirty jokes at rehab. I would go visit many of my senior friends, sing to them, then tell a few jokes to make people laugh. I found that it brought me a lot of joy and contentment. My elder friends looked forward to my coming and visiting, because I was getting very good at my dry humor. But this new part of me was not anything that my family knew of, and trying to deescalate all the anger, I threw in a badly timed joke. He did not find it funny and took it literally.

When he went to his room, I thought about all he had been through. He saw me on that bed, passed out and bloodied from hemorrhaging. He had no idea whether I was alive or dead. That is a strong scene for any 17-year-old. Samuel had dreams of becoming a preacher and going to college. He was probably feeling like he would end up like Gladys, taking care of me till I got better, putting his college and preaching dreams on hold. I wanted him to fulfill his dreams too. I went to his room and told him he could go live with Mr. Gabriel if he would have him. I called Gabriel the following day and he agreed.

Samuel left in a huff. For months after, I would only see him at church when the babies and I were picked up by Gabriel. Samuel would act as if he did not know me; as if I was not his mother. I was deeply hurt. Gabriel said he was still angry over my leaving and being gone for four months. Many times, I tried to talk to him to see what I could do to make him feel better, but he continued to refuse to talk to me.

I went through the same thing with his sisters. None of them would accept my calls or emails. Both wanted me to leave them alone. Gladys was constantly insisting that I respect her boundaries. I did not understand what she meant or why. It was extremely hurtful and confusing. But I found Gabriel was acting the same way. He would not take my calls or my texts and insisted that I not call during work, after work, or on the weekends. Okay, that meant never. But why? What had I done so wrong? He used the same words as Gladys; respect his boundaries.

Why was I suddenly being walled out by everyone? At the church, people did not want to sit near me. In the choir, the joke was made that I smelled, and no one wanted to sit next to me. At one point they had me practice with the choir in the foyer away from everyone. I cried for that whole practice and, eventually got up and called a taxi and went home. It was too humiliating. After three months of being home, I called my pastor wanting to talk with him. The change in lifestyle, the abandonment of my family and friends, the isolation; it all was breaking my heart. Is this how God saw me too: something so odious that he was isolating me away also? The church secretary refused to let me through to my pastor. I could not get his attention either. What is this, God? What is going on? Am I now at fault for being crippled also? I did not ask for this. Why is everyone running away from me?

Well, I was able to deceive the secretary into patching me through to my pastor. I begged him to please come to my house and speak with me. I did not understand what was happening with people's responses towards me, and it was hurting me very deeply. He agreed, and both he and the associate pastor came to my home. I expected my pastor to say something comforting or go through the Bible in some way to help me accept being crippled and work towards getting better. I even thought maybe he would come and tell me about how people's responses towards me were natural, and for me to have patience and mercy towards them; some grace. But he got straight to the point and said people did not feel comfortable worshipping with me, then he got quiet and looked at me as if he was afraid to say it.

"Someone as disabled as I am," I said.

"Well, like you said," he replied. "You would do better not to come to church but to stay home and catch services on livestream. It would be better for everyone."

Then the associate pastor said, "Let us pray." Two minutes later they were gone from my home.

I have no words to speak how utterly broken I became that day. I thought, is this how God sees me? This is what God thinks of me? He made me and formed me and breathed the breath of life into me. Why? Why had he allowed me to live through all that I have and to become broken as I presently was? Was it all a joke? In my crying and complaining to Gabriel, who was attempting to avoid me as best as he could, I tried to look back and see where it was that I became cursed. I thought when God saved me, the curse was washed away. I thought Christ had taken all my sins upon Himself and they were no more, because I was now justified through the shed blood of Jesus Christ. And I was, but when did the curse get placed back on me? Where in my life did I fail God to where he could have nothing more to do with me? Where was I missing it?

I thought all the way back to that first night Jacob came home from the war and asked to make love to me. I said no. I was not ready. I quickly got his wrath when he hit me hard to the floor then dragged me to our room. I believed that night was the night I defied not only my husband, but God. From that day forward, I was cursed. The curse had always been on me. That is why all these things happened: the domestic violence, Howard raping my family and others in our community, being locked up in a psychiatric ward against my will, the homelessness, the loss of my money, my children turning away from me and ghosting me, the loss of my health, and being cut off from life. Now even my pastor and my church had rejected me and cut me off.

This was not the first time a church cut me off. When Howard was arrested and arraigned, I tried going to my church for services, hoping I would find solace and comfort there. But the incident was in the papers and everyone knew what my husband had done. No one wanted to sit with me or talk to me. I lost some my best friends at the time. I was not allowed to serve in Sunday school or the choir. That first Sunday back, after services, the elders came up to me as a team and asked me not to return. They said they transferred my membership to another church. So, the following Sunday I went to the church my membership had been transferred to, and I was met in the hall before going into the sanctuary. I was asked to leave and told no one felt comfortable with me being there.

The little ones and I were completely on our own. Life seemed very dark and empty for us as I tried to live without God. While I was in rehab, the nurses would use me to help encourage the other patients. I was not getting paid, but you would have thought I was working with the staff. Before I left, one of them gave me a card and suggested I call the International Fellowship of Chaplains.

"If ever I met someone who had the heart of a chaplain, it is you."

When I got home, I called. They had a training in Georgia coming up and they invited me to come and join them and find out if this was where God wanted me to be. How could I become a chaplain and be used by God, when God was making it clear, He did not want me? It seemed like He did not love me anymore.

"Gabriel, am I cursed? Has God cursed me? Why have all these things happened to me?" Gabriel had no answers for me. At one point I asked to meet him at the church to talk about why God had cursed me. "Could you show me in the Bible what someone could do if they are cursed by God? Can God take it away, remove it? I want to get back to life. I have never been able to live a life for myself and do the things I wanted to do. I have always been held back by fear, obligations, and the demands of others. I dutifully fulfilled all my duties and obligations. Even after the Howard incident, I paid and bought my children back; I provided a home and schooling for them; I put them first. I went back and learned to drive so I could take them to their AP courses outside our school jurisdiction, and I took them to their games and music recitals. I worked extra hours to pay for field trips, instruments, dances, and summer camps. Was it not enough? What did I need to do more? Show me in scripture what I am missing?"

Gabriel and I made a date to meet one evening at the church. I showed up and waited for him. He never came and gave no reason why he did not.

When my father's inheritance came through for all of us, it was less than we all expected. Brian was the executor of the will and he tried to take all the inheritance for himself. It became a six-year battle in court ended by my Aunt Carol. She hired her own lawyer and fought Brian on the behalf of the Cinnamon family, my mother's people. In the end, after lawyers' fees, the over $200,000 all of us should have obtained was reduced to $25,000. This caused an extreme rift in our family. Gabriel came to me when the inheritance was mailed to me and insisted I give him half of it. He said he deserved it because he had always been there for me, helping me without one dime. And now I should give him what was his. I gave him 10 percent. My adult children wanted their part too and expected me to give the inheritance over to them. This I did not. I told them they had what they needed, and I was going to use the inheritance towards me and the little ones, as my future was very unsure. They were angered by my answer.

There were other people who suddenly wanted to be my friend again and hoped I would give them part of my inheritance. When it became clear that that was not going to happen, they disappeared again and went back to refusing to talk to me, treating me as if I had leprosy.

Like an avalanche, the people that were closest to me began to walk away from me. Gabriel no longer wanted to talk to me nor associate with me, other than to fulfill his obligations as my "guardian," not as friends. Through tears, I begged him not to leave.

"Please stay. I need my friend Gabriel. I need you. I cannot be alone. Please."

I depended on him so much. I put all my dependency in him and not God. I would have panic attacks if, for one moment, it seemed he would no longer be my friend. He stayed, though he did not want to.

My adult children came to my home the weekend we were supposed to take Samuel to college, and they let me know how they felt about me and why they were deciding to divorce themselves from me. They said I reminded them of the past and they did not want to live in the past anymore. Without thinking, I angerly yelled, "If you do not want to be my children, then don't."

Realizing my anger got the best of me before I thought about it, I quickly said "Wait a minute. I did not mean that."

But by that time, they had gotten up and walked out the door going to their car. It took me awhile to get out of my chair and follow them out the door. Gabriel stood in the way of the door and would not let me go outside after them. I did not understand why. I tried to call them on my cell phone, but they would not pick up. I begged Gabriel to let me use his cell phone, but he refused. I was crying and screaming for my children, but it was like Gabriel was deaf and blind to my agony. Finally, he let me call on his phone, and Gladys picked up. I apologized for letting my thoughts come out so quickly like that. I did not mean what I said. They were my children and I loved them. But no one seemed to care what I had to say. They hung up.

For weeks, I did nothing but grieve. Anna and Emmanuel would sit or lay with me in my bed, and we would cry and sleep together. There was no reason for life anymore. I considered some form of suicide for all of us. Then there came a knock on my door. It was Samantha. By this time, Samantha had changed her life around. She was once a bully at school and dated a lot of boys. We were friends and sang in her mother's community choir, but that did not hold Samantha back from having a reputation. She was very pretty and attractive and loved to go out and party. At some point in her life, God got a hold of her and she gave her life to Christ. From that point on, she lived for the Lord, and like her mom, she became a strong prayer warrior. She was studying to become a pastor when she showed up at my door. Word had gotten around that I was no longer in church.

"Why go to church if God has cursed you?" I said. "He does not love me anymore. I am nothing to Him. If I go out that door, bad things seem to always happen. We are safer here at home."

"Vicky, you know better than that," Samantha replied. "God did not curse you; He loves you. He gave you Jesus. All these things that have happened to you; so what? You think God does not know? He does. He has a reason for allowing them. I do not know His reason; I am not God. What I do know is that God cannot call Himself a loving God if He has cursed you, or anyone else for that matter. You are only cursed if you choose to reject Jesus. Have you rejected Jesus?"

"No, of course not."

"Then you are not cursed. When is the last time you read from the Bible?" I did not want to answer that question. It had been a long time and I was embarrassed to admit it.

"It has been years, Samantha. I cannot bring myself to open the Bible and read it. I am afraid of all the judgment I will get out of it. It's enough that everyone is judging me."

"Judging you, about what?"

"Howard, having Anna and Emmanuel…"

"I'm not judging you. Howard was not your fault. You married a man who did not love you and was a criminal. Did you know he was a criminal and did not love you?"

"No, I thought he was the answer to my prayers and my rightful husband after Jacob had proven to be a disappointment."

"You got that right. None of us have come to terms with how much he had changed. But Vicky, God does not hate you because of Howard. Howard did bad things. He did not love Jesus, or he would not have done what he did. Howard was a bad man. That does not make you bad. He took advantage of you and the children. You did not know those things were going to happen. Howard knew what he was doing. He drugged you and he hurt the children. Now your family is broken. You think God does not know that? God is a healer and a way maker, Vicky. He can heal your family and make a way for your family to be whole again."

"But why, Samantha? Why would God let all of this happen? Why me?"

"Why *not* you, Vicky? What makes you so special? Nothing. We all are living through crises and hard difficulties. Everyone has disabilities they must live with. Look at my husband. He broke his back while in the military. He lives with disability. I was date-raped as a young lady. It brought me to Christ and caused me to grow up, but I live with the brokenness of what was done to me. You do not know what someone's challenges are, so you cannot assume yours are the worst or the only ones.

I do not know why God allows bad things to happen to people, except that He uses those bad things to get our attention. He loves us and wants the best for us. He wants us to live victoriously justified by the cross work of Christ and living under the covering of His love. God can and will bless you, provide for you, and love you through your circumstances. But you must trust Him and turn to Him for your every need."

We prayed together and she invited me to her church. I learned that God will bless me, provide for me, and love me through my circumstances.

CHAPTER FIFTEEN

Judas Betrayed Jesus With A Kiss

"Two tickets to Georgia, please."

I was on a journey to discover what it was to live a life completely trusting God and no one else. Going to Georgia, a place that was a thousand miles away from the safety and familiarity of my home, surrounded by complete strangers, riding on the filthiest of buses to an unknown event where I could possibly be rejected, with very little next to nothing in my pocket.

"I know you are scared about coming," the chaplain said. "You are choosing to leave your comfort zone and go where God is calling you. That is part of the work of the ministry. When we pray to God about what He would have us to do for His glory, He will make it very clear what His will is. Then it is up to us to choose to obey or disobey. I am not pressuring you, Vicky, but I honestly hope to see you here. And if you do not come, we won't love you any less, sister, and neither will God."

I did get down on my knees and pray about whether God wanted me to do this, or if this was just me dreaming grandiose about myself. I had had large ideas before, but I rarely acted on them. I could not leave my children; so many things I did not do. I did not want to be embarrassed if it did not work out, so a lot of dreams I let go of. I would ask the advice of Gabriel, Gary, my pastor, or others. Most of the time they would tell me how much of a bad idea it was, unpractical, or just plain foolish. So I would not go. This time, God clearly told me to go. I wrestled with Him about how I did not have enough money, I was too crippled to do this, I had no transportation to get there, I could not go anywhere by myself anymore because of my brain injury, what would I do with the children, what if they reject me; but God clearly said go. They were all against my trip to Georgia. They saw me as being foolish and unwilling to accept being disabled and my new normal.

"Father, I repent of so much. I have made so many mistakes and I have been lost for a long time. I am so afraid of making another terrible mistake, God. I do not want to do that. I want my children to be happy. I want to be safe and content. I want to serve you, God, but only if my family is well and not wounded in the process. I want to do your will in my life, Father, but not at the cost of my family or my own integrity. I am asking you to protect me, Father; protect my children. Please give me wisdom to be able to do your will. Show me which way you would have me to go, and I will follow. Show me through your word how to obediently serve you in my life and the life of my children, so I

might mentor others and be a demonstration of your merciful love towards us. I am trusting you, Father, because I know I can. Whatever you choose for me in Your will, I will obey you and I will follow you. I recant all of the things I have done, said, and thought in the past that did not glorify you. I ask for your forgiveness for my willful disobedience, and I seek your face to do only what you would have me to do. I love you, Father, and I thank you for loving me so much. Amen."

Over and over, God would tell me to go. He provided the child care, the transportation, a little bit of money, and an escort. So I went. When I got into Georgia, we were dropped off in the middle of Atlanta on the street at 1 a.m. I was terrified. Mr. Fritz did the best he could to protect me. Then I did something outside myself. I stopped being afraid. I looked at the people on the street as people instead of danger. One of the street people who had been pacing and talking to himself came up to me. I was a little scared, but I asked God to protect me and keep my heart open. The man asked me if I needed a ride. We said, yes we did. He waved down a taxi and got us a ride. We offered him money, but he wanted nothing. He just wanted to do something good so God would bless him. This was my first test of trusting God, and not myself. God truly was a way maker, my protector, and my provider, and I was learning to trust in Him.

We used the little bit of money we had to take a taxi to a hotel. The driver insisted I give him more than what the ride was worth, or he would drop us off in the woods in the dark. With no choice, I gave him double the amount. When we showed up at the hotel after 3 a.m., I did not have enough for the two rooms I had reserved. No one was at the desk, so we sat down and waited. What would I tell Mr. Fritz? He will think I was stupid for having done this. The new church we just started attending would think the worst of me. I would be a failure again. Then I stopped myself and the flood of negative thoughts.

God, please help us. We are stuck. I do not have enough money. The cab driver wanted more than I should have given him. I am sorry; we did not know what to do. I did not ask for your help. Well, I am now. Please help us to get a room with the little we have, God. Amen.

As I was praying, an older chubby woman came in looking around for the attendant. She looked very troubled. She found a seat beside me and settled into the chair like she had walked a thousand miles.

"Hello," I said.

"Hello," she said back.

"How are you doing?" I asked. She opened like an unread book. As if she had been waiting to dump her heavy burden on someone, she shared how she was there for the funeral of her mother. Her mother was her best friend and she would greatly miss her. She wanted God to give her back, and wondered how was she going to live without her.

"One day at a time. One moment, one second, slowly, you will get used to her not being there," I said. "It is going to hurt a lot. You will cry a lot, and there will be a lot of days you will not want to get up and live. But get up and do the everyday things you need to do to live. Do not put your mother away, but rather, remember her every day. Think on

the good and wonderful things you both used to do together. Find some of the memories that made you both laugh. Cherish everything about her, so that when things get hard, you can go back to those good memories, and they can make you feel better. We cannot get our loved ones back when they leave us, but we can hold on to the memories and let those memories comfort us and reassure us. We can one day go to our loved ones when our life is over. Your life is not over. God has a wonderful work He wants you to do still, so go do it. He will get you through this pain. You will not always hurt this bad, only for a moment. But those wonderful memories, they will last you for your entire life."

She hugged me for a long time and cried. Then she forced a wad of money into my hand.

"Oh no, you looked like you needed someone to encourage you. I do not want your money. Consider the counseling session free," I smiled, hoping she caught my joke.

"You didn't have to listen to me," she said, "Please, just keep it." She got up and proceeded up the steps to the next floor.

"Aren't you waiting for the attendant?"

"No, I have a room already. I just could not sleep, and I went for a walk. You really helped me. I can go to sleep now," And she disappeared up the steps. Shortly after, the attendant came in.

"I'm so sorry, I fell asleep in the back. Don't tell anyone." he joked. When I put my money together with the lady's money, it was exactly what I needed for the two rooms, nothing less.

"Ma'am, I am sorry, but we had to give your reserved rooms away. But if you wait for a moment, I will get you two more," So we waited a little longer. In the end, he was able to get us one new room. I did not know why God would want us to have one room together, but at least we had a room. The next day, with no money to get transportation over to the training center, we stood outside of the hotel trying to figure out what to do. A gentleman pulled up in an eighteen-wheeler and got out. He stretched for a while and noticed us standing in front of the hotel.

"Good morning, are you okay?" he asked. Mr. Fritz went over to the truck driver and talked with him. He signaled for me to come over.

"We have a ride," Mr. Fritz said as the truck driver picked me up and placed me in the cabin of his truck. Mr. Fritz folded my walker up and got into the cabin himself. The truck driver grew up at the church that the training was being held at. He felt honored to take another chaplain candidate to his home church. When we showed up and interrupted the class that had been proceeding for fifteen minutes, the trainers were surprised and stunned that it was me and that I came in a walker.

When class was over, we were given a ride back to our hotel room.

"Do you have any food or need any rides?" I told her yes, I did. The chaplaincy made sure for the week I was there that we had food to eat and transportation back and forth to the training. A chaplain gave us the 30-mile ride back to the bus station at the end of the training and made sure I had some money in my pocket for any expenses that might come up going home. By the time I returned home and sat once again on the side of my bed, I was stunned by the lesson of faith I just learned. I did not trust in myself or in the people around me. I completely trusted God to provide for me and He did.

During that time, I began to grow once again as a person and a Christian. I followed the counsel of some of the chaplains to begin again as a Christian as if I had been saved for the first time. I began to read the Bible all the way through once more, and I was in school online for my bachelor's degree. This allowed me to dig deep into the doctrines of our faith and apply my faith in my everyday actions. Because I had never been baptized when I came to Christ in 1986, I was baptized with my son Emmanuel in August of 2017. I also changed my name to Victoria Angel, signifying the death of my old life and the family curse that held my family back for so long. Never again would I take another drink; never again would there be violence in my home; never again would I place my dependency on people; never again would I live for anyone else but Christ. I took a stand: "This curse ends today!" The changing of my name was my proclamation to God's sanctification within my life.

In November of 2017, my family and I had traveled by car to San Antonio, Texas, for training and to participate in praying for those who had lost family members in a recent shooting. My housing officer called me to inform me I had lost my Section 8 voucher. She did not understand why I had not responded to her warning letters for the last six weeks. I told her I had received none. Gabriel received all my important mail from housing and from social workers.

The housing officer apologized for calling me and making me upset. She told me to enjoy my vacation and she would handle things from there.

I got off the phone with her and began to pray with the other chaplains that were in the room and heard the developing concern. Then I gave a call to Gabriel. He got on the phone and yelled at me, not realizing he was on speaker phone. I tried to ask him about the problem housing brought up to me. He denied knowing anything and yelled at me for interrupting him at work. I let him know he was on speaker phone and the chaplains were in the room listening. He promptly cussed me out and let me know what he thought of me and my chaplaincy. I hung the phone up on him so he would stop embarrassing himself. I came home six days later. The housing office had Gabriel charged with adult abuse and neglect. They removed him from off my case and had the police sent out to investigate him. In one swoop, my hero, my guardian angel, my mentor that I had looked up to for so long, was gone. Again, I sat on the side of my bed wondering what God was doing. How would I survive without my best friend?

Gabriel had not used my money to pay my bills for over six months. He left a trail of massive debt with my utilities, rent, the private school I was still paying on, and my insurance. Paperwork for my health insurance and housing had gone uncompleted and missing. Many forms had my signature on them when he and I sat down to complete them, but they were never turned in when Gabriel had offered to turn them in. The funds I gave him from my disability check to pay my bills and concerns were never completely used on all my bills. What he did with my money, I do not know to this day. But the money I had entrusted into his hands, he never applied to my bills.

I learned from the investigator that not only had he not been paying on my bills or turning in important paperwork to housing and social services, but he falsely filled out paperwork having me listed as being paranoid schizophrenic, he witnessed to many that I was dangerous and should not be parenting my children, and he had made several attempts to take the children and foster care them for the state. He also was among the list of many family members who had called Child Protective Services since 2010 (16 times in all) accusing me of being a child abuser. Each time was unfounded, but it was so excessive that it led to an investigation into the main callers. Gabriel was one of the main callers.

The thing that troubled Social Services the most was whether I knew that Gabriel was a felon. He had two counts of felony on his record for sodomy behavior and attempting to pick up a young adult for sex in the parks. Gabriel had no business around me or around my children. God protected and saved me and my younger children from a fate that could have mirrored Howard. I let my Superman, my archangel, my mentor, my Judas Iscariot go, and I finally placed my dependency completely on God.

Dear Gabriel Wonder,
We saw all of you outside of the Olive Garden on Sunday as we left. I chose not to look at any of you. It

made me angry. Once in the car, the children started crying again. Anytime we see you or your name is brought up, the children cry. I cry. Your name is never brought up. Our hurt is that deep.

It took me years to be able to write, let alone form the words that I need to say to you. But trying is always a better option than quitting, and I want my healing. So, this letter is not for you, but for me.

Sometimes I wish you could feel the hurt and pain of abuse and betrayal that you put me through. But then, I truly do not want another soul to ever know this kind of soul wounding like you inflicted on me.

I have held onto this pain for years since you tried to pull me out my front door, almost causing me to fall. You got in my face and yelled at me as if I was garbage. I never expected that from one who I saw as my best friend, my brother and mentor, the one I looked up to and called my guardian angel. I always believed you were something more than you appeared to be, Superman. But you took advantage of my trust and innocence until you destroyed me. In your destruction, you wounded my children.

You thought you were powerful because I looked up to you and trusted my life in your hands. You thought I was weak because I needed support; because I was disabled and alone. I trusted you; I followed you; I listened to you; I thought nothing but good of you. I defended you in 2007, and I prayed for you and went out of my way to care about you, because that is what love does.

The truth is you were never powerful. All power belongs to God and his children. Evil has no power. You thought me weak, and you did not think well of me. You talked evil of me to others, and you plotted my harm with others. You did not care about my person or my soul. You hated me, but wore a façade of love I did not see through till it was almost too late.

You tried to make us homeless; you tried to steal my children; you tried to put me away; you tried to destroy my good name; you pretended to be my friend when you were my enemy. You made me the butt of your jokes, and you despised me. You took my trust and hatefully abused it before others for your own gain and the building up of your own name. You took the hearts of my children, and you twisted their innocence and naivety and muddied it with your hatred and bitterness for your own life. You used their trust of you to commit wicked acts on your behalf, and you sat back and laughed at their ignorance and lack of wisdom and knowledge. But not once did you count the cost of the bruises you were inflicting onto your own soul and the path of destruction you were creating for yourself. Not once did you give any thought to the murder you were attempting to commit of my life and others.

I would be lying if I told you I never thought about revenge. My mind wandered there many a times, but my demons never got the better of me. Love will not allow that. Love does not retaliate; it does not think evil of others; it is not proudful or vain. Love believes all things; love never fails. I cannot sink to your level, or I would be just like you, and I do not want to be anything like you. I do not want my children to see me as a reflection of you, someone who is two-faced and dishonest about who they are and their intentions.

I have wondered, do people always do these things to the ones they love? I have wondered if maybe I do not know what love is. You said many times, in your own words, if I were not the way I am, we would get along better, it would be easier to love me and care instead of feeling apathetic and indifferent. You would always have an excuse for yelling at me, cutting me off, not answering the phone, claiming not to know when bad things happened, dismissing, not caring but going through the motions, lying about not taking part in things that never made sense. You always said these were my fault, and I believed you to the point of believing myself cursed. You were okay with that.

But I do not believe these lies anymore. I chose to stop blaming myself for what was never my fault. You are responsible for your own actions and emotions, not me. Your apathy and indifference were a red flag of something dark in your own heart you needed to go before God and handle, not point a finger at me. Your willingness to jeopardize my life, my stability, my home, and my family out of apathetic spite and bitter hate and indifference was a sign of a lack of a personal relationship with Jesus Christ in you and a loss of the work of sanctification in you. Somewhere along the line, you walked away from God, and Satan played havoc with your soul. That is not my fault; that is yours. You are responsible for your heart and your soul so that the hearts and souls God places in your care (myself) do not get hurt through you. You squandered God's precious gift of grace in your life, and you accepted Satan's tools of theft, murder, and destruction in their place. You stole away my children's hearts, you attempted to murder me, and you went out of your way to destroy all that I am and all I stand for: Jesus. What wounded you so badly as a child that as an adult, you would work so hard to abuse others?

I am not your excuse for being incapable of controlling your emotions or your excuse for being apathetic, bitter, and indifferent. I am not your narcissistic pride or your psychopathic fragile ego. I am not the weakness you believed you saw in me, nor any of the hateful names you called me in your jokes about me.

You do not define me. I define myself. I am more now than the marks you have left behind on my spiritual and my physical heart. I had another major stroke in December 2017. That damage became permanent. Despite it all, I press forward to be whom God called me to be. I have my degree, I am a chaplain, I will reach my destiny despite you and without you. But I will write about you one day. I learned many lessons because of you. I learned what God does not want me to be and how bitterness and hate can make a wonderful and amazing person—who you once were in my eyes—into something ugly. I do not want that for me or my children.

I hope one day you will turn back to God and renew your relationship with Him. I pray one day you will repent of your hate and anger and stop making excuses for the sins that you commit in the dark. Man may not know one of them, but God knows them all and He is no respecter of persons. Your sins will find you out, lest you repent and turn back to the God who made you and loves you. When that day does come, I will be long gone, and it will be too late for you to reach out to tell me that you are sorry.

Right now, I pray God help me to forgive you for destroying my family. God help me to forgive you for dividing my family and leading my children astray. I pray God help me to forgive you for being negligent with my care and my life. God help me to forgive you for trying to hurt me physically at my house. God help me to forgive you for trying to cause us to lose our home, for besmearing my good name publicly, for making promises and commitments you never intended to keep. I forgive you for leading me to believe you loved me as family, when you never loved me at all. I forgive you because I want to be free.

I say these things in the name of my Lord and Savior,

Jesus Christ.

CHAPTER SIXTEEN

And This Is How We Love

It had been three years, and there he was getting out of an apple red car in his Ford mechanic uniform. The car did not look like it was his; rather, it looked like he was working on it, which was his usual business. I sat there in my brother's car, in the drive-thru at Kentucky Fried Chicken, and just stared in disbelief. On the day that we had gone down to the DMV in Manassas and chewed out the supervisor who had reinstated my driver's license, only to suspend it once more for no reason while we were away on vacation in Florida; out of the blue, there stood Gabriel Wonder III.

I could not stop staring. The first thing my mind thought was, there is my guardian angel. I wanted to jump out of the car and run to him and hug him and say, "Where have you been? I have missed you." But very quickly as if my true Guardian Angel had slapped me sorely across the face, that fleeting thought left me and in its place was the deepest contempt. I just could not stop staring, my heart was screaming "How could you, how could you!" My heart cried out, "God, why is he alive? Why is he still standing there? Are you not the Great Judge? Why have you not struck him down and burned him to a crisp? Did you not see what he did? Do you not know what he has done to my family? It is ruined by this thief, this monster, this Judas, and yet here he still stands! Is this justice? Is this right? Strike him, God, I am waiting. Just strike him!"

Then suddenly, as if he could hear the screaming voice of my soul, he turned his head on those broad shoulders, squinted, and looked directly at me. He looked surprised, too, and stood there for a moment as if expecting me to jump out of the car and race towards him to beat him to death, or worse to blow his head off with some sort of gun. He stood there with an unnatural smirk on his face, the mask that fooled me all these years completely removed, and arrogantly waited for the retribution he deserved at my hands. But instead, I just sat there and stared at him with the deepest hatred, pain, and hurt that any human could know, and I did absolutely nothing. My soul fell to its knees in my head and cried bitterly.

After a while, as if he saw all my sorrow and pain as weakness, he dismissively saluted me then turned around and continued to work on the broken-down car he had come out of. Soon it was our turn in line and we drove past him till he was out of sight. My brother Nathan saw him, too. "Just ignore him," he said. We got our fast food and went on. When I had finished writing this book and placed it in my editor's hands, I did not give any thought to my past any more until that day. It was too coincidental me running into him like that.

Well, as my editor was working on my book, he came upon what I would like to call a "misspoke" I made while I was writing. I believe that as a writer in order to write from your heart, whether it be fictional or nonfiction, one should let the thoughts freely flow onto the page and make all the grammatical errors as you will. I can fix all those mistakes later, but what I must share, I cannot pull that out of my heart again once my heart has spoken it. So, I let the voice of my heart speak and fix the mistakes later.

So honestly, my editor had a lot of work ahead of him, and he was worth every penny I paid him and more. However, he stumbled upon a mistake I made about forgiving my father. The way I wrote it, it appeared as if I still held a grudge towards my dad for all the painful and hurtful things he had said and done throughout my life. It seemed as if I had not forgiven him, and my editor, being the good Christian "Daniel" that he is, did not think twice about admonishing and encouraging his client about the important of forgiveness in God's children. If I am, and I am, God's daughter, a child of the Almighty God Himself, then I will forgive my father no matter what because my Father in heaven has forgiven me no matter what. Our God, the King of the whole universe, is the ultimate judge and sovereign of us all. And if I love my God as I profess to, to the point that I am willing to humbly write this book about my life, publicly laying myself out bare before all so that others can learn from me and turn away from evil, repent, and worship the one true God in all purity and holiness, then who am I not to forgive a child of the King that is precious to Him. I wrote him back and told him honestly not to be afraid, I had forgiven my father, and God gave me the chance before my father passed away to tell him. I had a father, my father was saved, he was a child of God. And I had a father, a human father for three months, who loved me and told me he loved me for the first time and only time in my life, and I knew it. I watched this hardened man, this sadistic, sick man, go from being Saul to being a Paul. And as if God knew how hard it would be for him to be a Paul in this world, and how tempting it would be to him to turn back, God took him home. But God showed both of us mercy and grace by allowing us to be father and daughter for three months.

So no, I hold no grudge against my father, and I praise my Father in heaven for healing our wounds together before my father passed. Yet, on this day, as we drove out of the drive-thru at KFC, and I watched him drive away in that little red car back to the Ford dealership; I recognized I had never forgiven Gabriel for what he did to me and my family, and despite writing this book, I found that day that I was struggling to forgive him. That day God revealed to me that though the wounds of my father were healed, the wounds of my ex-husbands were healed, even the wounds of what Howard the monster had done were healed, the wounds of Gabriel Wonder III never healed, and I felt ashamed.

Back in January 2018 I was struggling with forgiveness. My psychotherapist and I met twice a week to work on my learning to forgive others for the things that had happened in the past. During Christmas break I endured another stroke, and it left my left arm and hand limp and weak. I could not use it. I could not lift anything. When I tried to use it, I dropped things easily. I was bumping into doors and walls and falling for no reason and I could not get up anymore. I had come so far with my recovery from the third stroke in 2016 only to be set back again in 2018. This time I was sent to physical therapy three times a week. Now I had a new task, forgiving myself, forgiving my body, and forgiving others. I did not want to, but I knew I was at a crossroads. Bitterness was begging to return. Because I have been down this road before, I knew where it would lead: anger, bitterness, hate, and eventually apathy and hopelessness. All that leads into the valley of death: suicide. I did not want to go there.

But for the first time in a long time, I was forced to deal with my emotions and my mental anguish without the support of a bad habit such as alcohol, starving myself, binge eating, dumping my cares on others expecting them to fix it, or overspending money I did not have to spend. For the first time since belonging to Calvary Chapel of Washington, DC, I was forced to lean on the savior of my soul, Jesus Christ, and I was scared. We had become acquaintances, not family. I found that just praying with my hands folded and eyes closed simply did not work. Even when I went to the emotionally charged church I eventually joined after leaving Dale City Baptist Church, all the tears and singing and emotions just did not touch the struggle I was fighting inside my heart. My soul was at war with the enemy, and I was losing.

Strokes are funny little bugs because they let you keep some things, and they take other things away. By this time, I could not share scripture by heart like I once did. I could remember pieces, sometimes I even remembered chapters and versus in a book, but I could not remember the words. The words were just hanging there on the tip of my tongue out of reach. It was as if I could hear my soul reciting chapters and chapters of scripture like I once could so long ago, but I could not get the words to come out of my mouth and it hurt so much. Many times, during service or when I sang with the choir, I would break down and cry because I longed to have his words come out of my mouth again so freely as they did in my younger days. So, I learned to stop being so formal with the Lord and I just started talking to him like you would a friend standing beside you.

Somehow this stroke removed a lot of my inhibitions and well, in a matter of speaking, I let God have it. What I mean is I started arguing with God and yelling at Him and telling Him how angry I was with Him, with my body, and with everyone else, and how could He allow all this mess, and, well, God take it and place it where the moon does not shine! Now, I do not suggest that anyone decide to talk to God in this manner. To be honest with you, I did do a lot of cussing, and I honestly say please do not follow my example in talking to God this way. But I think God purposely stripped me of my puritan ways when it came to prayer and worship so that I would learn to be sincere and childlike, as God wants his children to be when we come to him with our problems. The more I angered and raged out at God, the better and healthier I slowly became and the easier it became to forgive and to let go of the past.

One thing my counselor and I worked on as I worked my way through AA's three-step book was how to put forgiveness into practice. I realized that it was time for me to learn how to forgive freely for real. I began to go back to my adult children and others from my past, and if I was able to forgive them face-to-face or ask them to forgive me face-to-face, this I did. Those that I could not ask forgiveness of face-to-face—whether it be because of distance or because they were deceased, or because it would bring more harm if we met face-to-face—for whatever reason, I just wrote letters. And as I went through this process which took some time, God slowly healed my heart and opened me up to a world I never knew. He slowly stripped away my fears and the things that had held me back for so long. I was winning the war over agoraphobia and anxiety. I was slaying depression and elevating age-old wounds that had never healed.

But do not fool yourself into thinking it was that easy; it was not. God had a bigger plan for me in the area of forgiveness before he ever intended me to conquer the obstacle called Gabriel Wonder III.

In January of 2018, I finally got the guts up to go knock on Gary Harris's door. I brought my oldest son along with me just in case anything happened. I had practiced what I was going to say repeatedly in my mirror and rehearsed with my counselor. No matter what he did, I was not going to react but to think first, stay calm, forgive him sincerely, and ask him to forgive me where I had been wrong. When he opened the door, and invited us in, I was surprised. I expected him to burst out in anger, as he had the last time we saw each other. Instead, he broke out in tears and ask if we could start all over again as friends and see where it would lead. I was taken aback. This was too easy, and he still seemed to care about me. We both fell back into our relationship where we had left off, as if all the ugliness of 2015 had never happened. In fact, he outlined a plan he had been working on to return my van that he had stolen from me after he had enough money from his new job to purchase a car of his own. It all sounded too good to me, as if God heard the deep want within my heart.

I loved Gary more than I had loved any other man, and I recognized that, although I felt no romantic or intimate connection with anyone else—man or woman—like one would when in love with a soul mate or a lover, I loved Gary that deeply and no one else. As we drove away from his house, I felt euphoric as if God were rewarding me for doing this difficult work called forgiveness. What I did not realize was that God had just put the test paper down in front of me, started the clock, and told me to begin.

Within a four-month time, Gary was basically at my house almost every day, all day. We were peanut butter and jelly once again. We held all things in common. Both of us seemed to believe the same things spiritually, politically, economically, and socially. Our conversations on life were so deep and long, I felt satisfied as if this were what my heart had desired for so long: someone who knew me, and someone I could share my heart and my life with. I felt like I found my Adam and that I was his Eve. We still had our arguments and our disagreements, but we seemed so much more connected than we had before 2015.

I found myself beginning to lean on him and depend on him. I found myself shortening my conversations with God and elongating my conversations with Gary. Soon he began to go to my new church; he also began to take my time away from my studies in school and insulted my work as a chaplain.

I did not like these negatives; however, I put up with them because I did not want to let him go. I did not want to be alone again. So I endured the negatives and kept moving forward. But all these things kept happening. Once I got my van back, it kept breaking down in odd ways. But every time, God found a way to fix the problems at half the normal cost. Where we lived at the apartment, I was running into problems with my neighbors that I did not have before. The police were nightly showing up at my home answering the accusation of us being too noisy. Problem was, we were not. When we lived at the house, the landlord that I seemed to get along with so well turned her face against me and threw us out even at the risk of being removed from the Section 8 housing list. That house sat for two years before they were able to get someone to move into it again. Then there were those times my service dog Isaac suddenly disappeared for no reason. It was unexplainable and heartbreaking. Each time, we eventually would get him back, but his disappearing never made any sense. Then the people at the church we were attending started acting strangely towards me and my children. It was unsettling and we did not understand why. I could not put my finger on it. It felt like people knew a secret about me that no one was saying anything about, but I always had that feeling I was being talked about and looked down upon in a negative and derogatory way.

When Gary finally asked me to marry him, he seemed to change, too. It was as if becoming engaged to me gave him the freedom to take his mask off. Not one day went by that he was not yelling at me and arguing with me over everything. Everything I did and said was wrong, and it was my fault that he was unhappy. I felt so little and incapable, like I needed to do more to make him happy. He stopped dressing nice and started dressing filthily and sloppily. He ate without etiquette now and talked to me in a demeaning and insulting way, both publicly and privately. My heart was taking a beating on the daily. I found myself preaching to him daily, and yet I was not even listening to my own words. I just did not want to let him go, even though everything screamed, "Let him go!" We were headed down that abusive road and it was time for me to get out.

And even though I was effectively debating with him over the authenticity and inerrancy of scripture and the Trinity of the Godhead, Gary began to go down the slippery slope of false belief and mysticism to support his deviant carnal choices. I was not looking at how my choices to cling to another idol, Gary, was leading me to sin in my own thinking.

In the summer of August 2018, I had just finalized paperwork with my lawyer. I finally divorced Ken legally after thirteen years of marriage, ten of them being separation. That was another odd thing that occurred during that time. Ken and I had divorced shortly after separating in 2010. While engaged to Gary, I learned the divorce papers were never delivered to the court clerk for processing. For ten years Ken and I lived believing ourselves divorced. God was merciful to protect us both from making any relationship mistakes. Gary and I were in constant heated arguments over faith and lifestyle. And his roving eyes were not just looking at other women, but he was also looking at my daughter in inappropriate ways too. That last day, I think it was a Sunday, Gary in his anger tried to hit me, but I moved away before he could. He walked out of my room, and what I learned later from my son, he was met by my son holding the phone to his face and threatening to call the police if he did not leave.

Gary left for good. It took almost an hour for me to realize he was gone. I thought he went outside to cool off. I was ready to forgive quickly again, but only because I didn't want to be alone and I didn't want that humiliation and the shame of acknowledging publicly that my wedding was off and my fiancé was gone. But that was my reality, and I sunk down on my bed and bitterly cried. I did not cry because Gary was gone, and I did not cry because of the humiliation of my marriage dreams being dashed permanently. I had sunk down on my bed and cried because I recognized how quickly and easily I had gone so far away from God once more and quickly replaced him with another person.

It was God's mercy removing Gary before I made another fateful mistake, so I laid on my bed in tears. I was begging God to forgive me for straying away from Him once again. I was His prodigal daughter coming home, and I asked Him to please take me back, even if I just lived outside the gate of heaven. I'd rather cling to his pearly gates for the rest of my life then to dip my toenail into hell fire for all eternity. Instead, God blessed me over and abundantly. After a week of wallowing in my own despair, my brother Nathan took me out to the car dealership and helped me get a new car; my kind of car. I felt elated. And because I had graduated from my college with a B average, I was offered a scholarship to go to seminary school and achieve my master's degree. I took it. Along with that, the Department for Aging and Rehabilitative Services (DARS) program finally came through and got me a job at Pizza Hut behind a cash register. There was not a day that went by that I did not go home without a large tip. I was not even a waitress, yet people wanted to tip me because they liked my friendly nature. I found I really enjoyed working there with the young people. I started going to a divorce group and to AA meetings, and I began to work on the difficult areas in my life that I had avoided dealing with.

The week Gary left me, I got a knock on my door. It was raining outside. There stood two angels. These young girls were Mormons, and they were soaking wet. I invited them in to dry off. The one reached out and hugged me for the longest time. I truly needed that hug more than food. That began a lasting friendship with people I found to be very dear. Though I am not a Mormon, I learned that God truly visits us when we need Him the most, and in the most unexpected ways.

I was passing God's test, I believed, and I was really feeling good about it. I had good friends once more, and all of us did a lot of things together. I felt so liberated. All the pain of before seemed to be no more. I could talk about the past and think about it without crying and hurting over it. I was working on renewing my relationship with my older kids. I still could not reach Samuel and Rachel, but I felt positive about the future. I really believed things would get better. I had stepped into a higher plateau and understanding of God, and I felt I was maturing and becoming wiser.

One day driving my car down the road with the kids, I had excruciating pain in my side. I felt woozy and sick and I did not know what to do. I pulled the car to the side and we went into the McDonald's. I sat down on the bench and laid my head on the table and that is as far as I could go. I was burning up and sweat was pouring down my back, yet I was shaking and very cold. My son recognized something was wrong and asked the cashier to call 911. They took me to the hospital, admitted me, and informed me I was passing kidney stones and I had a bad bacterial infection. After about three days I came home weak, like I had given birth to boulders, but it was bearable.

We went to the National Zoo in DC with our friends, John and Shana. I went in my wheelchair. I got out of my wheelchair and stood up with the kids while we took pictures in the panda frame. When we were done, I went to get back into my wheelchair but forgot that the frame went across, in front of me, so I tripped and fell flat on my face and palms of my hands and knees. I was bruised up badly. I went to the hospital again with contusions to my face, the side of my leg, the side of my arm, and the palms of my hands, as well as on my forehead. It took a couple of weeks for the pain and swelling to go down.

During that time of being tender to the touch, Nathan came home from work running a high fever. It was December of 2019, the time that people normally get sick with the flu. However, my brother Nathan was known for never getting sick. Yet here he was sick with what they were calling at the time the "super bug," a strain of flu that was new and unknown and hard to get over. At the time they were hinting that it came from China. Nathan could not breathe, his chest was congested, he ran high fevers, sweated, had body shakes, vomited, and had diarrhea like nothing I have never seen. Then four days later, I got sick too in the same way. Both of us were so sick that it was literally painful to attempt to get up out of the bed or even to raise our voices or to breathe hard.

I cannot describe the body pain or the struggle to breathe. The tenderness from the healing contusions made me want to exchange my body for someone else's. I cannot describe how much it hurt to vomit repeatedly. I did not want food. Oddly enough I could not taste it or smell it, so I did not want it. We both ended up in the hospital. We were advised to go home, take the antibiotics, lots of fluid and Pedialyte, and to get plenty of rest and ride it out. And if our fevers spiked higher than 102, come back in. So, we both lay in our separate rooms for the first few weeks, weak as lambs and drained of all strength. There were days of unimaginable high fevers and dry heaves, and other days of just struggling to get a breath out. Both of my children looked fearful, and Emmanuel would come lay on my belly not wanting me to go anywhere. So I crossed out going back to the emergency room. Instead, I let him and his sister experiment with cooking in the kitchen and playing nurse to Mom and Uncle Nathan, giving us our medicine. After a while, we started to get better, the biotics did what they had to do, and Pedialyte gave us energy when we could not eat any food. But it would be five months before either of us could taste food once more or even smell it.

In March of 2020, the world stopped. Everything that we had ever known came to an end. We were all mandated by our government to shelter in our homes for an indefinite period because we had been hit by a worldwide pandemic. I could go on in this book and talk about the riots, the looting, the fear of police that was instilled in us, the heated political climate that all of us John Q's were thrown into unwillingly, the lack of proper schooling and education for children, and even the mental health issues that presently rage through our children and even in my own home as a result of the forced isolation, the unnatural separation from each other socially, and the dark unfriendly climate that has settled within our homes, our communities, and even in our churches. But I would be going beyond the scope of this book, and that is not my intent.

Living through all this present ugliness and unsurety has thrown me to my knees daily before the throne of God and has left me dependent on riding on his strong shoulders, because I can no longer walk on my own two feet. But more importantly, it has shown me that there are still areas in my life that need fixing. And I believe this is the point of the test that He set before me back in 2018. It was not about whether I would choose Gary over Him, but whether I would choose to trust Him and whether I would depend on Him, whether I understood what was going on around me or not. I chose people over the God of the universe! That is insane, but we do this every day. The God of the universe patiently waits for us to come to our senses and recognize that we need Him in order to live.

As I and my family are struggling to survive through this new world order that has begun, this is what I am learning: to obey is better than sacrifice. And I say to my Heavenly Father: one moment in Your palace is better than one thousand years without You. To know You, my God, are pleased with me and that I have done well in Your sight up against all impossible obstacles is more important to me than any comfort that gold, money, or silver could ever buy or pretend to give. Therefore, I am writing this final chapter to admit that I am learning to forgive Gabriel Wonder III for all the things he had done and is still doing in my life today, as I slowly discover all of it. However, daily my Father is healing my heart and helping me to come closer to that point of forgiving my darkest enemy, because the truth is that man is not our enemy. Satan is. And Satan will use people who are closest to us to steal our hearts away, to break those heart strings, and to clog up our valves with the waste of sin. He will rob our peace from us and try to destroy us utterly. But God says no. No, because Satan does not have the power to destroy us utterly, nor does he have the power to steal our souls away from God.

God says, "Take my yoke upon you, for it is easy and light." He says for us to rest under the banner of His love and He will shelter us under His wings, for He loves us so. And He says He will judge; He said "Vengeance is mine; I shall repay." Therefore, I do not have to be afraid or forever fester in pain inflicted upon me. He keeps my life secure in the palm of His hand, and I cannot lose it unless I give it away myself. Therefore, He calls us all, and He calls me, to trust Him and obey. So though my flesh is weak, and Satan tries to sift me like wheat, my spirit is strong, and I hold on to the anchor of my soul. And where my flesh refuses to forgive, my soul says "No, God, help me to forgive and to trust in Your justice, for You are true and every man is a liar."

So, Gabriel, if ever one day you pick up this book and read it, May God forgive you for everything you did and said and all the damage you created. May God save you from yourself and from our enemy, Satan, and give you eternal life. And I pray all blessing and peace upon you, and pray that God will humble you and draw you to repentance to His glory forever. Amen.

In the writing of this book, I learned the best way to win over those whom you believe are your enemies—and the best way to obtain vengeance over those who you believe are Judases in your life—is by one way: to love. And how is that applied? The Father taught us that this is love, to love your God with all your heart, with all your mind, and with all your soul, and to love your neighbor as yourself. All the commandments are summed up in this. If we are willing to love each other in this way, despite the ugly things we do and say to each other as human beings, not only will God forgive us, but you will achieve the ultimate revenge over others. This is love. This is what Jesus came to show us, to teach us, and to demonstrate. He set the example. This is what He calls us to do as well, nothing less.